LIFE OF A SUICIDAL AMERICAN

LANDON MITCHELL

Strategic Book Publishing and Rights Co.

Strategic Book Publishing and Rights Co., LLC
USA | Singapore
www.sbpra.net

For information about special discounts for bulk purchases, please contact Strategic Book Publishing and Rights Co., LLC Special Sales, at bookorder@sbpra.net.

ISBN: 978-1-62857-674-0

Dedicated to the memory of Roxcie Ann Mitchell
aka RAM

If not for the genuine love and kindness you and Doris P. Mitchell raised me with, I may not have made it this far in life. You instilled the values and morals that I strive to follow in an America designed by the devil to tempt me around every corner. If not for the thought you gave me that God would not have created us just to have us destroy ourselves or each other, I may not be here today. Between the fiery emotions of rage during times of injustice, tempting me to strike down those that wronged me, or the devil's best friends in self-pity, sadness, and doubt, I could have easily taken my own life, or someone else's, as I see being done daily in the news. I have tried to live my life the right way in a world of wrongs, and it is the memory of you and my faith in God that you laid the foundation for that keeps me on the straight and narrow. I will always have the memories of you and Doris in my heart to guide me through the remainder of my life. You could have been selfish and had the television raise me, but you loved me and cared for me and taught me, giving me the mind-set to succeed and to see the lighthouse from the rough waters. Mother, you are the only perfect soul I have met in this life, and I know for a fact that you made it through God's gates and into that beautiful heaven that you spoke of so often. I love you and always will. I hope to always be that perfect son you always thought me to be. Thank you so much for the love, kindness, honesty, and the many other virtues you gave me. I will strive to pass them on as best I can.

CONTENTS

PART I

How We Got There

I am a bit of a history buff and firmly believe in the adage that those who forget history will be doomed to repeat it. The truth of that thought is painfully obvious to me as I look and see the same mistakes made over and over, with everything from world leadership and currency to religion and freedom, all intertwined and following similar cycles. I myself can draw a parallel between my life and this great country of ours in the twentieth century. My teens were guided by those that were older, stronger, and more knowledgeable than me. My twenties were a blur and roaring with good times full of drugs and alcohol and lost memories. My thirties were full of regret, depression, sadness, and hard times. I gave up drinking and wondered how I made it this far with nothing to show. My forties started off rocky and questionable, with other people forcing me to make hard decisions but leveled out with me on top and an occasional drink to celebrate. My fifties will be filled with peace, joy, and security, my sixties with freedom and love, my seventies and eighties full of drugs and good times and, should I make it to the late nineties or turn the century mark, my bubble will burst, putting me right back where I began.

The following is the story of my life as I perceived it, and it is all true, to the best of my knowledge, with nothing made up for dramatic effect. I did rewrite some parts to take out excessive, aggressive R-rated language and be more of a role model for those who may read it. If you absolutely hate the book, feel free to email me at ignorance_equals_slavery@yahoo.com and I will do my best to send you a signed hardback or digital copy of my attempt at fiction, *2038*, a self-published collection of short stories and scrap that I wrote when I was twenty to thirty-eight. If you don't like it either, then we will just chalk it up to another waste of money on something you thought you would like at the time, aka American consumerism. I think that is fair, as it has many wise quotes, interesting story lines, and a chance to find actual, real buried treasure! Now that my conscious is clear and I have plugged my other book, let's dig into the life of a *Suicidal American*.

In my early years life was great! I grew up in an upper-middle-class atmosphere in which I got most everything I wanted. My father, with the help of a loan from my mother's father, started a beer distributorship in a small, wholesome town called Brownwood in the middle of the great state of Texas. In under a decade he grew it into a three-million-dollar business. I was eleven at the time. I had lots of friends and almost everything a kid could want, at least when I wasn't grounded for misbehaving. Then my father decided to invest in an upside-down golf course in which the government had liens against. The government wanted to shut the whole thing down and sell it for what they could, whereas my father wanted to make the golf course work! The battle that ensued left my father bankrupt and suicidal. This I later learned from my mother, and, with my recollection of the events, I am certain is true. My mother turned to religion, and my father turned to another woman who had money, and he turned his back on his family.

I took care of my mother without electricity or running water in the heat of a Texas summer (June, July, and August). When this happened I felt like my father had taken the easy way out and hated him for this. I did not speak to him for three years. Looking back, I am grateful for this other woman, as my father was on the verge of suicide and I believe Vanessa (the other woman) actually saved him and allowed him a mulligan of sorts or a do-over. The easy way out actually would have been the suicide that he contemplated. After spending the summer of my graduation with no electricity and taking care of my mother, who had no one else to turn to, I did the unthinkable, I called her mother (the one she had not talked to in ten years because she chose her husband over them during a fight I was too young to know anything about or really understand).

They helped where I couldn't and took my mother and gave her a place to live and took care of her. When her mother passed at the turn of the century, she was able to help her stepfather around the house with cleaning and cooking. They helped each other, and personally I don't think either could have made it without the other. My father, on the other hand, made others perceive him as a millionaire again, but he never truly seemed happy—content, but never happy. A three-million-dollar mansion comes with a lot of burden attached (he would brag about how the property taxes were $50,000 a year, more than I made in eighteen months at the time). He had neighbors that he did not know and rooms that stayed empty for months, with very little to no decorations or pictures. I had to get his permission before the guard at the gate would even let me in. (What was I going to do, toilet paper his trees?) I personally don't see the allure of such a huge house for just two people. I would rather have a cozy house. Now maybe when I have five children I will be begging for a larger house, I'm sure, or if I had a group of friends who lived with me for my billiards room, because it is no fun when you are playing alone. A grotto is just a grotto unless others are there to enjoy it also. Wow! Five bathrooms, but all I need is one. Heck, I have enough trouble keeping it clean, plus, I know exactly where to find everything.

My mother lived in the country and knew all of her neighbors. She would get a call if a strange car was driving around or if something was out of place. The whole house was heated by a wood stove. Each room was wall-to-wall with pictures, dolls, and mementos, to the point that some would say it was cluttered. I say cozy, and I would much rather have cozy and full than empty and wasted. Lucky me, to be able to have two completely opposite roads to travel down. Some would ask, why couldn't you have both? I could have, but then I would be living a lie and could never find my true self. Who do you think is happier: A, the boy in a third-world country who has no toys and is playing tag with no knowledge of the toys in the world; or B, the American boy who has a closet full of toys but does not have the newest toy on the market that he sees advertised every day?

I will not lie or hide things from my mother, and let me tell you, I am, as my friend Anthony told me once, a master manipulator, something I learned from my father and others along the way. If I wanted to, I could walk around the truth with my mother, but by doing that I think I would be unable to genuinely enjoy my time with her. Besides, I don't even know if I have it in me to ever be dishonest with my mother, not to mention that I can't stand my dad's constant need to feed his ego, boast, and show off. He is constantly bragging about having the smallest camera in the world or using his OnStar in an attempt to impress his and my friends. I remember when he bought the damn house, he made a huge spectacle of it. He called my sister, her friends, and my friends and told them all to come over to see his new house! Okay, Dad, and so off we go to an empty ranch house where he was sweeping the front porch and asked us what we thought.

I immediately knew this was not my father's house and tried to go inside, which ended his little joke, if you want to call it that. Ha-ha, Dad, funny, for all you know my girlfriend grew up in a house half the size of that one, not to mention the fact I would have loved to have lived in that house. He took us on a few more twist and turns before amazing us with the three-million-dollar mansion in a gated community. (He leaned over to me and whispered it was a panty-dropper house: once they see the house their panties drop!)

Even back then, I was awake enough to know that I wanted to find my true love before I made money, because once you have money you can never honestly know if it is true love. Yep, learned that lesson from my dad back in '93-'94, when we went from rich to poor and my hundred friends turned into four—James, Chad, Shane, and a girlfriend, Katie, who would later cheat on me. After this experience, Rosa, my girlfriend at the time, fell in love with me, and I had to wonder, is she in love with me or the fact that I have a dad with a panty-dropper crib? I honestly feel it was the latter, but I will never know now.

I spent eight and a half years, on and off, working my way through school (something my dad said was mandatory to success in life, yet he paid for very little of it), granted, having a lot of fun along the way. I had just lost my best friend, Shane, because of a deceptive girl. They had been dating for half a year, and he really loved this girl from Massachusetts. We all lived together in the same apartment, and one night she came in when he was gone, and we started talking, as we had done many times in the past. She asked me if I wanted to lay with her, and I told her that I could not do that to my best friend. She was not happy and went to her room while I continued to play my video games.

The next day Shane woke me up and said in an angry voice that we needed to talk. He then told me how his girlfriend let him know how I tried to "force" her to have sex the previous night and that I needed to move out. I was heartbroken and tried to plead my case, to no avail. I can't say I blame him, as my high school sweetheart Katie was his girlfriend first, and although I asked his permission before we started dating, I could see how he saw a pattern, and he believed his girl and not me.

This was when I learned my lesson on perception. It is not the truth that matters in this world as much as it is what people per-ceive the truth to be. This is why I despise liars as much as I do and try my hardest to be honest in the devil's world. A wise man once said, "Perception is reality. If you are perceived to be something, you might as well be it because that's the truth in people's minds." This is why I see it important to live my life surrounded by people I can trust, even if that means my only friend is who I see in the mirror. My high school girlfriend ended up cheating on me, and the girl from Massachusetts ended up leaving Shane, so in the end what could have been a lifelong friendship was ruined in a blink of a lie.

When I first arrived at college I was humble and started school with a focus on my studies. My first two semesters I excelled, with a 3.7 and 4.0 GPA. Then I got a social life and became distracted. I graduated with a degree in marketing and a 2.6 GPA, with enough credit hours to have triple majored. I was ready for that $60,000 job that I was told would be at the end of the rainbow! What I got was a $14 an hour job being a restaurant and bar supervisor for a franchised Marriott near the airport. Nearly two years into my first real job I realized it was the same thing over and over again. Go to a building and work, go to another building and drink while bitching about work, go home and sleep and repeat the same steps the next day. After doing this for a while I thought, *Wow, grown-up life is so boring.* I went to college and came out with a pile of debt. Then I got the real job and did great! I turned my three departments from bottom 10 percent to top 10 percent in less than eighteen months! All this did was get me more responsibilities (two more departments, to be exact) and no raise and fewer friends as they were let go due to this increase in productivity from yours truly. Two years passed, and I had dinner with my father. I was excited that I had accumulated about $8,000 in savings and wanted to invest. Then I asked my father where I should invest: real estate, stocks, currency? He asked me how much I had saved. Wanting to look better, I told him $15,000, to which he laughed and said I should put it in my piggy bank and come back when I was serious.

It was this comment that made me feel life is just a mirage and I was a slave—two years for no pay raise and only $8,000? I quit my job a month later when I asked for a raise or extra benefits to compensate my extra duties. My general manager looked up at me and said, "It's not like you can find another job. We are in a recession, Landon. You need to get back to work before you get fired!"

I turned my two-week notice in immediately after that! I was so disgusted with the way corporate America works and was determined to succeed elsewhere. My direct boss, the assistant general manager, whom I liked, asked me to stay three weeks, and I agreed, yet I told them I would not train my replacement for them.

When my general manager, Nancy, said that to me, after all my hard work and success making her look good, I was hurt! I kept asking myself why such a heartless person, making so much money and doing so little, could treat me this way after I worked my ass off. I reached out to her superiors and told them of my experience and the lack of leadership in our general manager. When I checked in on my friends six months later, she was no longer with the hotel. I felt as if I may have made a difference. I often wonder why more of my coworkers don't speak up when they are treated wrong. When I posed this question to my friends, the most common answer was fear of being terminated or retaliation. When you live paycheck to paycheck it puts you in a position of fear and turns you into an obedient corporate slave. My favorite philosopher, Confucius, said, "If you look into your own heart and you find nothing wrong there, what is there to worry about? What is there to fear?"

I found myself driving to Austin and New Braunfels a lot to float in the river in my free time. So I decided to move to Austin as it was listed as America's number one economy and had the greenbelt, a huge maze of natural state parks, to visit. I was tired of the rat race, going from building to building and never seeing the sun much or actually enjoying life. It was as if my life had been on repeat since I graduated college, and it was wearing me down. It was tough transitioning from a Van Wilder fun time living day to day in college to a grown-up looking at and planning his future. It was like shifting from fifth gear to first, and this period started my battle with depression.

I moved temporally to Hutto, a small town just north of Austin, and rented a room from a stranger while I looked for a job. Then, after weeks of looking, I found a job in Bastrop working for Hyatt Lost Pines as a restaurant manager. Only six months into working there I got terminated for failure to report an injury that occurred on my third shift while I was still in training, five and a half months after the fact and after the associate refused to fill out an incident form because she said she was embarrassed and was not hurt, anyway. (She had been sitting on a glass rack that fell. I heard the bang, went into the room where everyone was laughing and she was blushing.) I had no idea this would come back to haunt me. I thought I had done the right thing. I asked her if she wanted to fill the documentation, and she said no, to just drop it. Turns out that this same young lady did not like being written up for being consistently late and blamed it on her injury that she received while hard at work. I was shocked to get terminated for this but was not too upset as I had money saved and hated the two and a half hours average driving time each day. After searching for a job that I felt I deserved for about six months, I decided to take a night audit position making $10 an hour, and then I got a job grading papers in the morning, just to get by. I was working seventy hours a week and barely able to stay afloat financially. (I never had to receive government aid.)

I worked both jobs until I was caught up on bills and then quit the day job grading papers for graduating high school seniors in Kansas. After reading over ten thousand essays I realized that the American educational system was broken and flawed and was releasing people into adulthood without the necessary skills to survive. The best analogy I can come up with is it would be like having malnourished slaves released into the Colosseum to fight well-trained Roman gladiators. It is a slaughterhouse for the rich and powerful to prey on, and young students don't stand a chance! Our public education system is a joke, and at best just teaches kids how to conform. I was living poor and starting to enjoy life a little more as a new friend, Josh Cole, showed me some fun things to do without spending much money.

Then one night my life changed. I randomly applied for a job as a restaurant manager at a nonprofit retirement home (Longhorn Village). I went on a few interviews and received an offer for $37,000. When I arrived at work I instantly felt at home, like this was my calling. I loved all the residents and enjoyed the staff I inherited, with the exception of my controlling, foot-dragging boss. I loved going to work. It felt like I was doing charity work and getting paid for it. In January, only six months after being hired, my boss was let go, making way for a new boss, Kevin.

I was excited when Kevin talked to me. He talked of good times and accomplishing things the foot-dragging boss never would have done. He worked hard and asked me to work harder. This I did, pulling twelve-hour days and working six to seven days a week. Again, I worked my ass off and, like Marriott, was rewarded with no raise, just more hours and more restaurants to manage. With Kevin's arrival I was given three more restaurants to manage, more stress, more hours, and less time off. I worked every holiday and did not call off sick for the first year! I only called in sick once in my entire employment with Longhorn Village. My boss had told me on many occasions that I was looking at an assistant F&B promotion in the final quarter of the year. Instead, I got terminated. Below is the letter I wrote to Kevin:

Kevin Holyfield,

I always thought you were a man of character. Now I realize you are just a master of manipulation. This comes from being denied unemployment because of lies and false paperwork (two write-ups) that I never saw, being put in my file under "refusal to sign." We both know this is a lie! I think we both know I was in the right when I got suspended by Chef on your vacation. Why else would you pay me for this and not further investigate or get my version of what happened?

In June, after you doubled my workload by giving me Tish's healthcare restaurants, I asked you for help keeping our associates in line as I was spread thin. Your answer to me was, "Fire one of the veterans. That will put them in line," with emphasis on Tucker. Then you left for a week. After much thought, I made the call to terminate Samantha, someone who was the ringleader of call offs, had all the documentation in her file, and was quitting in a month. If I had to do it, she was the one who deserved it the most and would be hurt the least, as she was already planning her move. I loved Samantha and hated doing this, but it seemed like you were right at the time. I had no idea the path you led me on here would have damaged my relationship with HR so badly.

When you left on vacation for a week this last time, you left Chef in charge, who quickly took the power and, without hearing me out, made a judgment against me, as I had raised red flags over him for violating the health code and for reusing food that had sat out for three hours longer than it should have. This is a major violation, and especially with the elderly here could result in fatalities! This is a nonprofit. Why are we breaking the health code to cut costs at the risk of the residents we serve? I thank you for coming to my defense, but I believe it was warranted. All I did was send home an associate whom I had asked to help us set up, and he told me no! I was unaware Chef had told them to not listen to me, which I could not believe after all the times I covered his ass, albeit to ensure resident satisfaction and not to cover his mistakes.

The only time I ever called in sick (once in seventeen months) you got upset with me and accused me of faking! You allowed me to work six to seven days a week, many for ten to twelve hours while dangling the carrot of promotion in front of me. You made me feel guilty for taking the only two back-to-back days off I had all summer! I worked twenty-six straight days after that, from July 4th through July 30th, without so much as a thank you. My August vacation request was denied, and my raise, although you spoke of me highly, did nothing to narrow the $18,000 gap between Chef and me. You took a career I absolutely loved and burnt me out to the point I could no longer smile genuinely.

When I got back from my well-deserved vacation time in October with my mother, I told you I needed more time with her and asked about FMLA or more possible vacation time to help her. You said you would look into it, just like you said you would look into the fact that I never got paid for the last five major holidays I worked! Now I realize you were just stalling and waiting for me to make a mistake, which came in the form of a person I considered to be a good friend in and out of work! When I took his drink away and told him to get back to work in a harsh tone, it hurt his feelings, and you played him perfectly! I get fired for sending a text saying, "How could you do this to me after all I have done for you? I see your true colors now, Friend." One text between friends is all y'all needed to send me on my way after all my hard work chasing that false carrot! Do you feel telling me the only way I can have two days off in a week is to get Sundays running perfect is a good motivation to put me in a good mood, while you sit back a thousand miles away from your family and wife and get your weekends off? I did what you asked when you asked, and yet you treat me like this? Where are your morals? Where is your character or compassion, Kevin? How do you justify lying to the TWC so that someone who worked so hard for you has no safety net to keep them from a complete tailspin? I hope someday you will realize.

Kevin, do you really feel I deserved to not get paid for my *one hundred and sixty hours of paid time off I had in my bank*? Or not to get a Xmas bonus when I was so close? Do you truly feel I deserved to have to wait five weeks for my last check? Do you feel I deserve to have my medications go from $75 to $439 because my COBRA paperwork never came? Does Clayton deserve to be homeless because I can't pay rent or find a job? Do I deserve that guilt? This could have all been avoided if you and Tammy would have been honest with the TWC and not lie about, not only the false write-ups, but the context of the text itself! LHV told TWC that I threatened him with his job and to take him to HR! This is a huge *lie* on your part and one that cost me being able to get by until I found another job. It will also more than likely put Clayton and me on the street and ruin our credit.

Thank You, Sir.

In conclusion, you took away the only job I truly ever loved, a job I loved going to. You made me a corporate pawn on your path to the top. You broke my heart times a hundred, sending me into the deepest depression I have ever been in (and without meds)! You lied to keep me from receiving the TWC lifeline I so desperately needed. I do share in the blame, as I allowed this to happen. Maybe it is karma for not doing enough to protect Pavla and Corin from the witch hunt you and Chef put them on. I'm not sure, but you have done a good job if taking the *heart* of LHV away and reinforcing the corporate $$$-only mentality that a nonprofit like LHV does not deserve. Start treating people from associates to residents the way you would want yourself and your family treated. Start being honest with others and yourself and God will reward you with a happy life. I'm not sure what God is wanting from me, but I believe he wants me to be thankful for the few things I have left.

With much regret,
Landon

If we are all energy, and we have a soul, then we can come back and try again. I think it's time to start over. Suicide is the answer! I need to kill myself and start over, bring my energy back and bring it back positive next time and do things differently next time around.

I really was lost at this point in my life. I had worked my ass off, just to get shat on again and again. Corporate America was playing whack-a-mole with me, and every time I felt I was gaining some momentum I got whacked back down to being a failure. I couldn't see a way for an honest man to make it up a ladder full of liars and cheats. I gave up, and, were it not for the fact that my mother instilled in me that the only unforgivable sin is to take life, I very well could have taken my own at this point in my life. Confucius says, "Our greatest glory is not in never falling, but in getting up every time we do." I had to keep going, but how? I did what I always do and looked to knowledge to fill my head in an attempt to step back up.

This is when I started reading *the Mystic Path* and finally figured out to kill my false self and to not allow my false self to bring the disease of negativity into my true self any longer. I gave my false self one final going away party and then took it all away. I suffocated myself, all those guilty little pleasures that provided me with a false since of happiness were taken away, and as sure as we need oxygen to breathe, our negative self needs these pleasures to keep us hypnotized into thinking we are truly happy! By taking away everything, I am suffocating my false self and all the negativity it feeds on. Now I am on my way to true happiness. I can see the joy and true happiness in ridding myself of all these pleasures.

However, I have a long road ahead of me before I can actually get to the point that I am truly happy. I just realized this as I went to look for a comedy to bring some laughter into my soul. I found a Redbox movie from a while back that I had failed to return. With my funds dwindling to the point that I can no longer pay the utility bills and have to gauge where I go based on funds available or gas, this was very upsetting to see that I had wasted money on this mistake. My initial reaction was that of disgust and anger, followed by that of questioning—how can I let this derail me after all the progress I had made? I frantically search for a cigarette and then find a quarter of one and smoke about four drags. I looked at my reactions, and the first was to get upset with the corporate structure. I thought, how can Redbox notify me every time I return a movie but fail to notify me when I have not returned one? The answer is corporate greed. Then I thought, how could Clayton have been so stupid to put another home movie on top of it, covering it up? Then I thought, wait a second, this is no one's fault but my own. I failed to return this movie because I was distracted with depression and all the things I was doing to get my mind off of how bad things were getting, and thus distracting me from this. I realized that I needed to step back and analyze my anger. Where did it come from? (My failure to return the movie.) Why did I get so angry? (My feeling of disgust over losing what little money I had.) How can I make this a positive? (By noticing what distractions I had around me and by realizing that being upset for a brief second serves a purpose of reminding me how easy it is to get off track.)

A week ago I would have gone to the store and bought a pack of smokes, wasting more money, and expressed my anger at others instead of seeing my own faults and let this quick negative thought consume me. Now I write it down and look at it as the first of many more tests on the way to true happiness! I firmly believe that if I can recognize the negativity when it hits, I can stop the chain reaction that will build momentum and revive my angry self.

I was able to calm myself within a minute with zero consequences. I look forward to a time when something like this cannot strike a negative vibe in me because of the powerful positive force inside me. I am going to have to work on training myself to stay positive, and I will reach that point of enlightenment I so desperately seek. There is nothing worse than my false self, allowing me to think I have reached inner peace, and yet it being an illusion. I must continue to analyze myself and my moods, to not *think* that I'm happy but to *be* happy! A good measure of this for me now is the amount of sleep I am getting. A week ago, at the height of my depression, I was sleeping eleven to fourteen hours a day. Now I'm between nine and eleven. I am on the last chapter of a Vernon Howard book, and I am excited to read it again. I still have doubts about my future, and I have anxiety, but these negative feelings are getting fewer and fewer each day.

Looking back, I wish I would have changed some things or left some things out of that letter. It really was crushing to find myself right back where I was just a few short years ago. To see the true happiness that I thought I could never find in a job just disappear, to have everyone I knew and cared about in the last two years just vanish. People I truly enjoyed being around, friends and people I looked up to as fathers I would have wanted to have. Looking back, you could make a case that twice my families have been completely stripped of everything due to the judgment of a few powerful people. My mother woke up from the first shock, and now I have awoken after this last shock! It's interesting to look back on myself and see a person who thought he was not judgmental at the time and see that I was. I believed my mother when she spoke of this experience. However, I never thought she reached the level I can now see. It's hard, I guess, for anyone to describe something so new when you have never experienced anything like it before. Vernon Howard makes an analogy of a mother trying to explain to her cub what it's like to swim. You just have to experience it yourself before you truly understand what it feels like.

Looking back on my great collapse of 2011, I allowed myself to let others influence my mood. In the past I had always dictated the mood, or I was able to release my tension somewhere. This time was different. I did not have a girlfriend or a close friend to vent to. I had a roommate that would agree with everything I said, which is the same as talking to the mirror. I did not have anyone to say, hey, let's get your mind off of this! Nope, I was stuck in a mental Alcatraz or a self-induced depression. I now see that I allowed myself to think negatively and feed off of this, allowing this negativity to grow and create more negativity. A good example of this snowball effect is when I was upset that I was working so much, 7 a.m. to 7 p.m., while my coworker who got paid 33 percent more worked 40 percent less. Well, one day I woke up and, in a hurry, was making a protein shake. When I took the lid off, it spilled everywhere! Instead of being thankful it didn't get on my suit, I snapped that it happened and kicked the stove! The stove shattered into a thousand pieces! I asked the apartment's owners how much it would cost to fix the oven's door. (The oven and stove both still worked. They just didn't look appealing.) They told me $500, when for $620 I could buy a new oven/stove. This angered me, and I told them they were being greedy and that I can't just, poof, fork over $500 that easy and refused to pay. I was already paying for the bathtub that they said I scuffed up. (This scuff was a huge crack that was there when I moved in. I just didn't mark it on my form as I was in a hurry). I went to pay rent. I wrote a check for the agreed upon rent, water, and bathtub charge. That same day the check was put on my door with a note saying it was $500 short and they could not accept it and that late fees would occur if I did not pay the full amount in two days. Wow! I was so angry. I saw it as corporate America trying to milk the honest American of everything they can!

I got up walked briskly into the office and shouted, "Why the fuck won't y'all accept my money?" In an act of intimidation, the apartment lady said she was going to call the police, and I said for what? She said disturbing the peace. I said, "What!? Do they send you to fucking conferences that teach you how to fuck people out of their hard-earned money and then to deal with it by calling the police? Who am I disturbing? Am I disturbing you, sir?" I asked the gentleman at the door.

He said no, albeit probably out of shock. Then I asked the other apartment sales rep, who was laughing the whole time, and she replied with a giggle, giggle, "NO!" She told me I was using foul language and that was enough to call the police! I got evicted a week later while I was on the only vacation I have ever had while working at LHV. Wow, downward spiral of negativity and that I actually handled really well. Once it hit the bottom I bounced high, although I think I had to, as my roommate was freaking out! I definitely think that his attitude made me have to tell him it's not the end of the world, it's okay, everything is going to work out. This is a good move! It worked for a bit. We got a new place and new neighbors and were happy for a while, until my negativity caught up to me at work. I would just let the negativity consume me and change my whole demeanor!

The mature people (that's the LHV politically correct way of saying retired people or, as I refer to them, friends) would often say, Landon, you wear your heart on your sleeve. What is wrong? Why couldn't I see this then? Maybe it needed to happen to get me to the place I needed to be. I am on the right path. Like Luke Skywalker in *Star Wars*, I can feel the force! I have no illusions that I have the knowledge required to obtain true happiness, but I do believe I have finally stepped down the right road.

I wanted a cigarette and just thought, *No, my false self wants a cigarette*, and my craving ceased. I wanted some ice cream, and again the desire was put away by seeing it as my false self! Now don't get me wrong, I haven't sworn off ice cream as evil by any means. I just realize it's a want or a desire that I no longer need to have! I am picking myself apart. I always thought of myself as being honest and morally correct, as a person who is a slave, or shall I say was a slave to his desires. Ice Cream, Pizza, Cigarettes, Gambling, Masturbation, Sex, and Television had me hypnotized into a false since of happiness! Now I enjoy the sounds of nature, the sunset, sometimes the sunrise, a good book, good company, silence, inner thoughts and examining myself. I feel so awake now, yet I still realize I have not broken through the depression completely, as I still see myself sleeping a lot and being anti-social.

It is hard for me to be social in a selfish society. Even something as small as going to the store is frustrating to me. On the way there someone pulls out in front of me and can't even attempt to speed up. I get to the store, and I can't park up front because the gray Dodge wants to park over the line, taking up two spots. I turn down multiple isles where shopping carts are unattended and blocking the isle. Why are people not considerate of others anymore? I'd rather just stay home where I won't have to see the selfish manner in which people conduct themselves in our society.

I see this as a transitional period, necessary for myself to get on the right path the correct way. It is very hard to give everything up like this without having negative emotions. So I decide to read and write, let the dopamine levels in my head quit spiking, and fight the demons, as some would say, in my own little world with no outside help. I have an interview on Wednesday, the fourth, and spent New Year's alone. On Saturday I smoked my last smoke, placed my last bet, ate my last pizza, my last pint of ice cream, and fantasized about women all day! My false self wanted one last hurrah, and I was very happy to oblige')

Then Sunday came and everything changed. It was a New Year and a New Me! I am writing this on Monday, or day two, a few hours away from day three. I have watched one movie a day, down from six a day at the height of my depression. No smokes. No gambling. No pizza. No ice cream. And I am doing just fine! I see it getting easier as I build momentum and feel like any day now I can break through the final wall of my depression and start living a positive, guilt-free life! I'm actually starting to look forward to the things I have taken for granted or had covered up with all the desires put forth in the big city. I can't wait to spend time with my mother and grandfather, help my mother walk again and chat with her about this newfound since of purpose. I am excited to move back home to the country, something that would have been the complete opposite had I not been enlightened! A few of my friends are telling me I can't give up and that I'm taking the easy way out.

(I know that's what my dad is thinking.) This is okay with me. Hell, I thought the same of my friend Nic a few years back. It is a hypnotized state of mind, one that thinks simple pleasures cannot bring true happiness, yet they do not see the negative in their comments. They do not see the positive in mine. They are brainwashed, and someday a great event will happen to them, and they hopefully will wake up too!

Watch the news and you get what a few powerful people want you to see. Watch a few channels and you may get a contrast of what a group of powerful people want you to see. But the truth, well, the truth is out there if you look hard enough, but beware, some people will do anything to keep the truth hidden. The same people who run the Federal Reserve also run the government and the media and the energy supply. We are all just slaves to the system we hold in such high regard. We just are too occupied with our own pleasures to wake up and see it! When the stock market crashed in 2008, they lied over and over again to prevent the slaves from panicking. When the rich and powerful screw up and fail, they get the government to bail them out with the taxpayers' (slaves') money. The national debt stayed under a three-trillion-dollar ceiling for its whole life until the last decade, in which it rose to fifteen trillion. The government can't even get close to balancing the budget. What would happen if the taxpayers got fed up, pardon the pun, and refused to pay taxes until we as a nation had a balanced budget? Chaos, that's what! Well, if the national deficit keeps rising at an alarming rate, chaos is going to peak its nasty little head out anyway!

The days go by slowly and painfully as I wait for a rescue of some sort, a miracle of some kind. Struck down from what I see as corporate greed and peoples' lack of morals and heart, I spent the last three months swirling in a downward spiral, destroying everything I worked so hard to recoup. I had spent my savings in an effort to rebuild my credit, fixed our apartment, and was finally satisfied with the décor. The next step was to find true love! With six weeks of vacation time saved up and the holidays approaching, I was sure I was going to find true happiness, fall in love, and start a family! Then one day I get derailed by losing my job, and not just any job, the job I actually love, the place I was planning on working until retirement, a nonprofit that would have paid off my student loans. I was so upset and frustrated with society. How could they just dump on me this way? How could they not have to pay me my vacation or unemployment? How can they let me just drown? I was drowning and failing and making things worse with emotions of self-pity, sorrow, anger, and sadness.

Day by day for three months, one hundred days, a quarter of a year, just locked in my room, in my own isolation. I am depressed beyond even that of my grandmother passing three years prior. I have many friends and a few family members that care about me so much and would have come to my rescue, but my fear of being a failure and my fear of bringing sorrow during a time of holiday cheer kept me from the few lifelines I had left. My roommate, whom I have been mentoring, had no idea how to react. Everything he said or did seemed to be wrong, and I slowly isolated myself from him. I just wanted to give up! I researched many religions, trying to search for purpose, the meaning of life, or why I'm here.

Then one day I picked up a book that answered so many questions and put the pieces back together for me. I have told my friends many times that poor people live happier lives than rich people, and that I experienced it myself. It was a debate that in the past I loved to have! So many hypnotized people pick rich right off the bat! No hesitation, but in actuality money does not bring happiness, if anything, it brings on misery, from what I have seen, at least. You see, poor people don't have all the access to the streaming media that hypnotizes your everyday individuals into slaves. The smallest things make them happy because they do not know all that they their missing. My good friend Anthony and I debated the fact that kids in third-world countries are receiving smartphones. I said I thought it was ridiculous that people in villages with one toilet and who are malnourished are getting smartphones. He countered that they can use the devices to learn and get an education, get out of poverty. My question to that is, at what cost? We could easily send people to teach, build, and help—hell, we do it to every country we invade after we destroy their government (Iraq, Grenada, Afghanistan). But if we give them smartphones we give them access to media! When a kid in a third-world country who has never had candy receives a piece of rock candy he is genuinely happy. When a kid in America who grew up with streaming media receives a piece of rock candy he is sad that it's not his favorite type and turns his nose up at it! We can live without 80 percent of what we have and be very happy! We work hard and stress ourselves out over things that corporate America and the government want us to be distracted by! They use these things to distract us from the truth! The truth is that we are just their slaves, and we are played like puppets on any given day.

I AM HERE FOR A PURPOSE: TO WAKE UP AS MANY PEOPLE AS I CAN FROM THEIR HYPNOTIZED SLUMBER!

You know what my mother, my grandmother, and the country taught me growing up? They taught me love, and that with love you can find true happiness! I remember so many truly happy times just playing canasta or spades, with the simplest of pleasures in life, knowing where you belong and being without judgment. The country taught me how to enjoy the simple life, singing with friends, exploring, being free.

You know what the big city, the wealthy, and my father taught me? These taught me that you can always do better, there will always be more. I remember from a young age having a father that always told me what I could have done better and rarely told me how great I really did! I remember that when we were wealthy we were never really happy, for some reason. We never really appreciated how good it was or were truly happy with the things we had because our eyes were also opened to new things, better things, and our want for these things kept us from truly enjoying the things we did have. It's like getting in your brand-new car and driving past a billboard for the new one coming out next month. You never enjoyed the new car because you knew there was a better one and it upset you that you didn't wait a month. The big city showed me that I was just a rat in a maze or a slave, for lack of better words, to society's rules and judgments.

Mother

My mother and I have been through a lot together, and I know she would never lie to me. Se dove into the Holy Bible during our family's bankruptcy in '95. Granted, she had always been spiritual, just not so 100 percent like she was from 1995 to 2000. Everything was about the Bible, and it turned me off! I would try again and again to talk to her, but no matter the subject, the Bible was turned to quickly, and a simple conversation would turn into a sermon. It was frustrating, and I didn't want to hear about it. I was too busy collecting my piece of the good old American pie, baby! I was distracted with popularity, new things, new friends, and all the glitter and fun of the big city. I was in the middle of it all. I quickly chalked my mother's spirituality up to how she dealt with the disaster of '95. It was not until I matured a little and she backed down to say 70 percent spirituality that I understood she had reached that elusive enlightenment, and not till very recently did I realize why.

Why my mother? Well, I knew she was a great person, but she too dabbled in luxury and excitement. Remember, she was married to my dad for twenty-four years, and he had a flare for the extravagant! My mother was distracted from seeing the light, as most would say, by her lifestyle. When her lifestyle changed and she gave up everything and wanted nothing, that's what put her in the prophet's enlightenment category! To believe 100 percent, to believe so much that you sacrifice everything and live in solitude, then you are among the likes of Edgar Cayce, Jesus, Mohamed, and Nostradamus. Then you truly see the light and are rewarded with gifts beyond the typical human being's understanding.

It just dawned on me after being in the country for less than a week that the biggest difference between the city and the country is that in the city you are always thinking about what you want. Everywhere you go you have advertisements and competition. I couldn't leave my house without having something thrown in my face saying, spend your money here! Hell, I couldn't even stay in my house without having solicitors coming to my place and trying to show me what I needed! I had stress every day because I was constantly needing more things, but I couldn't really enjoy them because of the stress I had trying to pay for them. I was smoking a pack a day because I was so stressed out. I was surrounded by fake people, and people that were really good at pretending to be real. Greed rules all in the big city, and loyalty and morals are for the weak!

In the country I find myself smoking two cigarettes a day and feel once I get settled I will give it up for sure! In the country I find myself relaxed and not wanting to spend money or smoke. I find myself to be much happier, as I am thankful for the things I have and the people I have to share them with. I walk outside and I think about my family and my life. There are no billboards, and when I go to town the billboards are for local businesses or eateries. I am not constantly distracted by flashy and fancy things. I can actually enjoy life as it is meant to be, and I am surrounded by neighbors that genuinely care about me. In the country loyalty and morals rule most, and greed is quickly weeded out! It is as if God is talking to me now through everything I do.

I watched a movie and my mind went straight to signs off my path. When I went to indulge in adult pleasures a great thunderstorm, the first in a year, struck down thunder and snapped me out of my lustful trance and back on the path, and my desire has yet to return. I open my Yahoo browser and go straight to the lead sports story: "Tebow Time: The 3:16 references." Then the story goes on to tell how Tim Tebow, famous for wearing John 3:16 eye black, passed for 316 yards, averaged 31.6 yards per pass, and, to top it off, had a final quarter TV rating of 31.6. (John 3:16 reads: "For God so loved the world that he gave his only son, that whoever believes in him shall not perish but have eternal life.") The scientific side of my brain wants to rack it up to coincidence, but my spiritual side knows it's guidance! In the past I would say I was just seeing these because that's where my mind was focusing. However, if that is true, then I'm focusing on God, and if he is guiding me then he truly is within, correct? I hope I can stay on this path and that this feeling of faith and correctness stays with me for the rest of my life!

Rhiannon

It was a few years into my college life and I was on top of the world,
it felt like. I had just come off of a 4.0 semester in which my high
school sweetheart had reemerged after cheating on me and breaking
my heart. I politely let her down and went on enjoying my life. I
had made many new friends without having to join a fraternity and
truly felt like the world was mine for the taking. We had a bar right
across the street from my apartment complex, called Hooligans that
we made into our nightly hangout.

Rhiannon was a bombshell blonde that had all the heads turning
when she walked in the room. She was a Hooters waitress with a
perfect body and large breasts. She caught my eye, like she did
everyone else, the first time I saw her. Seeing how everyone was
stepping on each other to garner her attention, I played the opposite and acted as if she did not exist. After a few nights she grew
bored with all the others and came over to talk to me. She asked me
why I wasn't interested in her. I told her she was all right and asked
if she was going to buy me a beer. She bought me a beer, and I
remember walking out that night alone. Unfortunately for me, I
don't remember those days that well. I remember being a dick to
her, and it drew her closer to me. I was constantly withholding the
urge to rip her clothes off and throw her up against the wall. It
wasn't until we held our Christmas party that I gave into temptation, and months of buildup led to a passionate minute of sex! I was
instantly addicted, and I believe she was also. She was rough around
the edges and had a lower-class upbringing, but I was never one to
judge on the past. I did not feel like I could bring her home to
Mother, but I felt like we could get her there, as she was very sub-
missive. We had a very fun and fast lifestyle in which we quickly fell
in love and had crazy passionate sex anywhere we wanted, anytime.
It was amazing, and things were great until I wanted to slow down
and she wanted to keep going full steam ahead. I overanalyzed the
situation, wondering if she was fit to eventually raise my children,

and, after many attempts to curb her drinking and drug use failed, I gave up on her—a decision I instantly and always regretted. I remember to this day the last straw that made me walk away was when I went to drink some water in the middle of the night and instead took a sip of her vodka. Instantly upset, I woke her up and said, "Rhiannon! What is this!?"

She replied, "Oh, that's mine, babe," and proceeded to chug a good five ounces of vodka and then went back to sleep. I thought, *There is no way I can have her raising my children, this just will not work.* The next day I broke things off with her, and, knowing that I was too weak to stay away from her, I up and left. For the next few years there was hardly a moment I didn't think of her, constantly wanting her to be around the corner or to surprise me. That day never came, and it was not until I saw her on Facebook, happy and with another man, that I gave up hope for a reunion of the beautiful blonde that stole my heart in my glory days.

My thinking was too selfish when I had her and too unselfish when I didn't! I truly wanted her to be happy, and when I saw that Facebook picture I believed she truly was. The crazy thing about Facebook is that very rarely are people what they seem to be. They always want you to see their new toys or their loving family, but it is very rare that they post publicly the sadness behind the photos. People are quick to say they have a new house or car, or that they fell in love. When they lose that love or the house or car it's very rare that they admit it publicly. I still remember holding out faith for a true-love fairytale life after seeing how happy my friends Wendy and Zack were. That faith was lost when I heard of their divorce. America has turned into a throwaway society of spoiled rotten, greedy people. You get something, and if you don't like it you just throw it away because you know there is plenty more afforded to you. If you think I am being harsh on Americans, remember that I include myself in my judgment. Honestly, we are!

I remember my grandparents reusing everything in many different ways. They wasted very little and valued everything they had. Not this generation. If it doesn't work or it has a stain on it just throw it away and get another. We do this with everything, from electronics and food, to relationships and friends. It is going to take a Great Depression, like that of the 1930s, to snap our society out of this euphoric self-righteous state that we are in. A depression keeps getting kicked down the road as our government keeps plunging us further in debt to keep the people happy.

When we went off of the gold standard and let a private organization with a government name dictate economic policy, we lost control! The only reason our money has value is because the world's resources are bought and sold using the almighty dollar. The wars that our country has fought this century have all been against countries that do not have a federal reserve banking system! Do the research and see for yourself! No matter what the excuse the government gives us—ruthless dictator, terrorist, human rights violations—the common denominator is that they do not have a federal reserve banking system that can be controlled. And that, my friend, is a risk to our society.

The history books will tell a much different story, but the reality is that America, the land of the free, is the country that is ridding the world of freedom from economic slavery. We are taught through the media that we are defending freedom, however, I have yet to hear through mainstream media that we are actually the ones that imprison more of its own people than any other country! Go ahead, I'll pause for you to Google it. Our grandparents grew up with a police force that was funded by taxpayer dollars and was actually there to help its citizens. We now have a police force that is run like a business and is taught to find anything it can to bring in revenue, revenue that then goes to buying fancy high-tech secondhand weaponry from defense contractors, like armored vehicles instead of body cameras, which I believe should be on anyone that has the authority to use lethal force!

So, the Mayberry police force can spend six figures on an armored vehicle, but they can't/won't spend $100 an officer to ensure the public is being treated right? The way I see it is that we are spending the money to fix the reaction to the problem (armored vehicles for riots) instead of fixing the problem (cameras on dirty police officers). I do not see America as racist, as most media outlets would like you to believe. I see it more as rich vs. poor class warfare. Is it fair that the rich can get away with murder while the poor are scared into taking a plea bargain? Do your research, but, last I checked, America has less than one percent of its cases actually go to trial! *Come again!* Maybe it's just the top one percent that go to trial, I don't know. The America I grew up in was all about having the right to be judged by your peers, yet the America I live in now is all about being judged by one person and his assistant. The way I see it, lawyers are just the modern-day version of slave traders. I know I am a little farfetched here, but they both brought poor people to rich people, made them sign a piece of paper, and got paid to walk away and not look back.

My best friend felt that his wife was cheating on him, so he followed her. She notices him and waves for him to pull over. He pulls behind her, and her new boyfriend pulls behind him. He gets out with a crowbar, as he is much smaller than the new boyfriend, and hits the truck, saying stay away from my fucking wife! Six months later, while they were still legally married, he was brought up on federal stalking charges, and after paying $10,000 to a lawyer he was told that if he did not accept the plea bargain he had a chance of going to jail for twenty years! He is now a felon, and I have learned not to move to a small town where your wife is from and that she can literally and figuratively fuck you! He is now officially a slave to America and does not have the right to vote or carry a firearm, and if he steps out of line he will be put in prison.

I'm not sure how I got on that rant, but for the flow of the book we will now go back to the love of my twenties, Rhiannon. She was a free spirit and always smiling. I always thought it was just her personality, but, looking back, I can't help but wonder if it was the stimuli from the drugs and alcohol. It was several years after we had broken up and not spoken except the casual Facebook happy birthday message that I learned she had taken her life through an overdose—a tragic American suicide that, like so many others, is overlooked in today's media as a mental health issue or common drug overdose.

Because of my love for her, I can see through this common conception and notice that it is the society that we live in that drives people to want to do drugs and escape. People want to escape the reality that is their life because of the way others treat them and look down on them and judge them. People give up on life because they do not have the life that Hollywood portrays or that they think their neighbor has because on social media they are so happy! People give up on their life because the grind in America is a ton harder than anyone wants to talk about. When things are going good, you turn from those in trouble, and when things are going bad, you turn from those that can help. Either way, the subject of what is fundamentally wrong with America is avoided.

I believe we have lost our values and our empathy toward each other. I believe our greed has brought us to the point that we no longer care for each other. Normally I would say I am different. I didn't drop my mother off in a nursing home and go on enjoying my life, like the normal greedy selfish American! I am a good guy! Except in the case of Rhiannon. I chased the love of my life into the arms of an enabler who sucked the life out of her until she couldn't take anymore and left this world only a third of the way through her life. I failed her and will forever have to remember the scars of her suicide.

My advice to you is that should you ever find someone that truly makes you happy and that you love, don't ever take that love for granted. Chase it with all the fire you have or be faced with the regret of forever having let it slip from your grasp, never to achieve the ecstasy of love again. When I was young, I told my parents that I wanted to run for president. When I was with Rhiannon, I told her I was going to run for congress. When she passed, all I wanted to do was run away.

PART II

Road Trip 2012

Day one of my road trip to Virginia with my mother and grandad was good! We got up early, around 6:30 a.m., and got to temple at 10:30 a.m. We enjoyed a meal at Yang Sings, and I had about thirty pieces of sushi! It was wonderful and definitely the highlight of my day. I quit smoking two days before, and the road trip was a great way for me not to have cravings. Granddad hit two curbs in Temple and two more during the night in Shreveport. His driving is getting worse, and I'm not sure how to get him to hang up his keys. I'm afraid it will have to take an accident for him to understand.

We passed a sign that said XXX books and porn movies, and my innocent mother says, "Hey look, a drive-in theater." My grandfather says we should drive through Corsicana instead of taking the loop around so we can see the city. I have never seen so much trash on people's porches in my life! The city reeked of sadness, and as we were looking around I felt sympathy for the people in the town.

As we left, Grandpa said, "See, if we took the loop we would have missed all that trash!" It was funny. We each had a burger off the Wendy's one-dollar menu, and it was nice. We are going to sleep, and I shall write more tomorrow.

On day two he pissed me off because we had discussed about a dozen times how it was a straight shot down I-20, and when I exited to use the bathroom, instead of saying something like, why are we stopping? Or bathroom break? He starts freaking out like I'm a retard and don't know what the fuck I'm doing! I slam on the breaks to where we can still get on the highway and yell, "I have to pee, damnit!"

"Oh well, no need to get all excited, son. I thought you made a mistake." Or aka, I thought you are a retard! Then later on, when he was driving (you see, I only get to drive the straight "retard-proof" roads), I needed to pee, and he says use a cup, here you go. I held it and about forty-five minutes later he starts complaining about Maggie (the dog) scratching his leg, and after telling her to quit about three times, he says, "Oh! She must have to pee."

That's what it is, Roxcie (my mother's name), she needs to pee, and he takes the first exit to accommodate the fucking dog! My mother (aka the retard's defense attorney) says, "Yeah, Landon does too!" To which Mr. Evil says, "Oh, I thought he had gone in a cup."

No, sir, I didn't. Not everyone is comfortable whipping their penis out two feet away from their mother, asshole! I thought this but did not say it; I just rushed to the restroom like a good retard.

The third day was rough, as it was raining, and Granddad almost killed us numerous times! (The scariest was when he went to change lanes and almost hit an eighteen-wheeler, then going fast up and down a mountain with little room for error he ran off the side three times.) I see his bitterness toward my mother and her handicap and it upsets me. I keep my mouth shut and try to make nice. The day after that we depart North Carolina and make it to the Virginia state line, and we are now sixty-five miles away from Grandmother's grave (the reason for the trip). We get in an argument, and he treats us like kids and says we should just go home! I was driving, mainly because I was unable to enjoy the mountains the day before because I feared for my mother's life and mine.

He had been complaining about his neck and back all day long, and I looked in the rearview and saw him stretching his neck really hard to see the dashboard. I say, "Granddad, if you want to know how fast I'm going I will tell you. You don't have to strain like that."

WOW! He threw a fit. "Landon, I'm not snooping on you, dam-nit! I could care less how fast you are going! You going to accuse of me blah, blah, blah." Then he said he was looking at the mpg, which I tried to explain was even smaller, and I was just trying to keep him from stretching awkwardly, and he was still pissed. Then Mother got pissed the whole time I was pissed. I felt he had no right to bitch me out yet again for something stupid.

My mother told him he was being ridiculous and to just be nice; she told me the same. He said he wanted to go home for the third or fourth time, to which I replied, "Okay, because that would make for a great story of how we drove fourteen hundred miles to put flowers on Grandmother's grave, only for you to throw a fit sixty miles away and turn around and drive home! Now that's comical and a great story either way, so okay, let's just go home. I can't wait to tell Lachelle (my sister) and James (his neighbor and only friend) about this."

He shut up, and we drove to Virginia Beach that night, bickering between him and my mother all night. When I got to the hotel in Virginia Beach, my mother and I were talking, mostly her venting about how she had to live with this man for so long like this and the stories. For some reason I just lost it! Right after she said, "What would you do if I were not alive?" I said I would commit suicide and went crazy punching the car over and over again, hurting my elbow as I slammed it into the side of the car. It hurts like hell as I sit here and type. The whole conversation made me think of my life and how she and spirituality was why I moved to Blanket, Texas! My negative side, that I have been trying to beat down, gained a hold over me and took over. I started thinking how hard it is to live with this old man and his strange and selfish behavior and how my mother puts more effort into making excuses on why not to work out rather than trying to work out and get better. I told her I have suffered enough in this life and I cannot sit by and watch her die! I lost it through a fit, totally out of control!

"Mother, I need you to be positive, fucking positive, and fucking trying to work on getting better! I can't sit back and fucking watch you rot away and die!" I yelled mean things as I know of no other way to get her motivated. I tried rewarding her with a foot massage after workouts. I call milk and eggs medicine as I know how important it is to intake protein to build back muscle. It's like helping someone that does not want help, like a drug addict or something. Her drug was faith and wanting a miraculous recovery to prove to everyone she has been right all along. I even told her a story about how a man on an island prayed to God for help as he was starving and couldn't take the hunger pangs anymore. When he awoke he had a small plant next to him. Instead of having faith in God, he looked at God as a prankster that was laughing at him for his own personal amusement. He then went to the top and jumped to his death on the rocks below. When he got to the gates of heaven he said, "Why won't you let me in?" God replied, "No faith, my son." The man replied, "I starved for eight days, then prayed for your help, and you mocked me."

God pointed down to the plant, which had grown in only a few days enough beans to feed a family of four. "Faith, my son," he replied, "you did not have, and without faith you may not enter. Faith is powerful, but it has to run alongside your own will!"

At the height of my anger fit I slammed the car door and went and lay down in the grass next to the water, staring at the moon, balling my eyes dry! The thought of my mother giving up and dying overwhelmed my emotions, to the point that I almost lost faith myself. (What kind of God would put us through a test this damn hard?) I have been good, not eaten any sweets, not smoked any cigs or pot, no masturbation or sex, no junk food! Been good for a week now in his name, and this is how he repays my love for him—with more heartache and a mother that won't help me help her and wants to give up? A grandfather that is spiteful and mean?

A father and sister that are materialistic? No female or life partner to walk this rough life with? Wow, you really test me hard, huh? Still I stick to the path as I tell myself that I am just on the final level of this game and that is why my test is so hard, for if it were easy heaven would be full of negative energy. I will stay the path, and as bad as I want a cigarette right now and know how easy I could get one just to calm down, I will resist the temptation of the false self and keep traveling down the path to Nirvana.

Day four of a hell of a road trip: It started off great as my mother got up and said, "Let's work out."

I guess my little temper tantrum had a positive effect besides positively making my elbow sore! Let's hope she does it again tomorrow☒ Let's see what the highlights were today: Well, we got honked at about thirty times, and that's no exaggeration but nothing new, as it's happened every day now. My top three fun moments were; number one, meeting Uncle Tommy, one of the nicest relatives I could ever want to have. He is a ninety-three-year-young cousin of my grandfather, and he lives by himself (his wife is in an Alzheimer's ward). He drives every day and is active in the community! He also keeps a spotless house. Wow, what a man! Number two was driving down to the shipyard and seeing the ocean and yachts. Number three was meeting my distant cousins at his hot dog restaurant. This is the son of the brother that my grandfather does not talk to (thirty years or so, now). He told me about how half the family is stubborn like my granddad and his father, and the other half have a reunion every year and enjoy each other's company.

My top three scariest moments of the day were: Number one, when my grandfather turned down a one-way street and stopped at the stop light to turn left. I said, "Granddad, you can't do this." To which he replied, "Oh Landon, be quite now. We are going back. I'm just a little lost!"

I said, "No Granddad, we are parked on the wrong side and

pointed to the other side of the median, where we should be.

He noticed this and backed up, almost hitting a tree twice! I asked if I could drive ten times, to no avail. Number two was when Granddad almost ran over a man in a parking lot he should have never been in to begin with! I was scared Granddad was going to hit the man at first, followed by fear that the man was going to drag Granddad out of the car. As he jumped back you could see the rage in his face. My mother waived her hands saying sorry, and my grandfather, never one to admit blame, yelling how the man was an idiot for crossing the parking lot. *Yes, sir, Granddad, those stop signs must have been for pedestrians, not cars, you asshole*, is what I thought ;) Number three was when we drove in water in the tunnel, and Granddad swerved into another lane. Fortunately, no other cars were there. He got pissed that Grandma's grave had tree roots growing through it, resulting in a tilting of the tombstone. On the way home that night, I got upset that my Mother had gone three miles without a seatbelt, and then Grandpa chips in with, "You're not worried about me not having one." To which I replied, "I don't know if it would help or hurt you more with your (interrupted with yeah, yeah, yeah, I know you only care about your) interrupted by me yelling, "Granddad, did you even hear what I said?"

He says, "I know you don't," interrupted by me in a harsh tone, saying, "Listen, you old goat, I said I didn't know if it would help you or hurt you because of your pacemaker thingy, but you don't care what people actually think or say, do you? You already have your mind made up with what your sick head wants, right?"

"No. No, I don't—"

"Yes, you do. This is the third time today you have done it!"

He replied, "Okay, okay, Landon, no need to get all upset. Let's just go back to the room.

To which I replied, "Thank you for lunch." Earlier we had got into it because he asked a lady if there was a Hobby Lobby to buy flowers for the grave. She said no, but there was a Michaels. I said,

"Great, Hobby Lobby and Michaels are the same thing."

He replied once again as if I'm an idiot, "No, they aren't, Landon. It's two different stores."

I and my mother (frustrating always having her defend me like I'm a retard) stated like the same kind of stores! I said, "Yeah, and they have coupons, make sure you grab the coupons at the front when you go in!"

Well, this pissed him off, and he yelled, "You think I'm trying to be cheap! I could care less about how much I'm spending." And he tore me a new asshole! I took it and could not understand how he misconstrued what I was saying. Then I realized he was just a prick and that's how they think. My mother told him on three separate occasions the correct way to go, to which he would reply, "Roxcie, you don't know. Just shut up and let me drive! I know where I'm going" He was wrong all three times, and she just took it, never rubbing it in. I sure did, though ☺.

We would drive down the street Mama grew up on and my mother would point to the place where she would get a soda and cream, and as she was describing how, he would interrupt with, "Look over there. That was where I would get my tires."

This infuriated me as he interrupted her very interesting stories with tidbits of information that I would not waste my extremely intelligent mind on, ever! I don't give a fuck where you parked your trailer, where you brought tires, or your first Plymouth! I do care about the shit of you so rudely interrupting consistently! He does not like my sister and has expressed his dislike many times, bringing it up sometimes three to five times a day that she does not care enough to call her mother and how lucky she is to have one as his was murdered at the age of fifteen. (His father had hugged him goodbye and told him to take care of his brothers and then sawed off a shotgun and went home to shoot his wife and then himself.) I try to explain to him about the distractions of her life and everything she has going on, but he does not care to understand. I even explained to him that she bought a phone that Mother never uses and that could hurt Lachelle's feelings. He doesn't understand texting at all. My mother said Lachelle was born at the blah, blah, blah, and he said I'm sure they tore that old place down! (Very spiteful), but hey, the fucking 7-Eleven that used to be a Goodyear he bought his tires at was worth driving past! We still don't know if the hospital Lachelle was born at is still there or not because he refused to drive the two blocks over and look. (Lachelle, this is the disease that makes his brain get stuck on something and play it on repeat. Sometimes I think this trip is more about his mother than his wife. He just won't talk about it. He loves you but just doesn't understand how things work in this age.)

I called him out on it, in a very polite way, by saying, "I'm sorry, Mother, go ahead," after listening to his BS and about a mile down the road past what she wanted to show me. Now that I taught him how rude he is, when my mother is talking now, he says, "I'm waiting until you are finished," about every three words, interrupting us even more! Spite is what it is, like when I did not want to go into Michaels after the whole "cheap" blowup and he tried to squish me by leaning his chair as far back as it would go. Fortunately for him I found it humorous, or we would be heading home now. I'm trying to figure out a way to piss him off just enough to head home but not enough that he hates me for it. He now says we will stay till Monday or Tuesday, so he can yell at the graveyard people about the tree roots. He does not understand how much it kills me to not have a job and how bad I want to get back to start my life from scratch for a third time.

Saturday:
Today was a good day, as Granddad and Mother both woke up in a pretty good mood! Mother wanted to do her workout, and Granddad wanted breakfast, so I told Mother to go ahead and shave her legs while we went downstairs and ate breakfast. Grandfather asked

me if he should take her a plate, and I said no sir, she is shaving her legs. We will have them make it toward the end of our breakfast, and the waitress agreed. She even said that way it will be hot! I told my grandfather that we did not need to say we were taking it to Mother, as he only had two breakfast coupons.

He replied, "She's in a wheelchair, Landon! She doesn't count."

I said, "What?"

And he said, "You know what I mean."

Well, I didn't understand that or why he took her breakfast up when I was complimenting the staff on their hotel. I went back to the table, and he had disappeared. When he later appeared, I said, "Where did you go?"

He said, "I took Roxcie her breakfast!"

To which I replied, "What?"

He said she was in the middle of shaving her legs, but she ate a piece of bacon, and she liked it! I asked why he did that and said do you not remember us discussing this a few minutes ago?

He replied, "Landon, they made it faster than I thought, and I'm eating my cereal. I didn't want it to get cold"

To which I replied, "So my mother gets to eat a cold breakfast?" He pretended he didn't hear. After this rude and selfish behavior, the morning went great. I did physical therapy with my mother, and then Uncle Tony came by the hotel around 11 a.m. He is the son of my granddad's only living brother and Helen, a kind, blind woman that he married and from what I hear is a wonderful person! She puts new flowers on all the graves and is really caring! Tony is a police officer and the most successful of the four brothers. He started describing his father, and it mirrored my grandfather perfectly! He said he is stubborn, something that runs in the Sumner bloodline; cheap to the point that he is embarrassed to go out to eat with him, and works every day, just like my granddad! He said if you didn't know they had a brother you would swear they were the same person, like twins!

Tony knew the most as he was the oldest of the brothers and remembered the dolls my grandma made and how my granddad would give the boys popsicles and show them how to work with tools, much like I remember, minus the popsicles. He had great stories about Franky, the cool brother who drank and smoked and partied. He told of how the others were stubborn and miserable, sad and lonely most of the time. He remembered a lot, to the point I referred to him as the family historian. He was fun because he put Granddad in his place and called him stubborn! He also would cut him off from interrupting and say, "I'm talking, you wait now!" I could tell he was used to what I am just now getting accustomed to.

When Tony had to take off, we went to accomplish our primary mission of visiting Grandmother's grave. Everyone was in a great mood after the visit with Tony, and they had already purchased the flowers the day before. Granddad was even contemplating reuniting with his brother, whom he had not spoken with in over thirty years. When we got to Grandma's grave he freaked out that the flowers were twice as big as the vase and bitched my mother out. We calmed him down only after I stated that he was happy when they got them the day before and that it was just as much his fault as he was there when they were purchased.

"I'm just upset, Landon! The damn flowers are twice as big as they need to be! Damnit, I told her ..." Blah, Blah, Blah! I went to the car, found a knife in his toolbox that was maybe eighty years old, and cut it in half. I said there is no reason to ruin a beautiful moment and argue in front of Grandmother! When he saw the flowers fit perfectly, he got better, although Mother was a little moody afterward!

The rest of the day shaped up great as we left the cemetery, at which grandfather pissed in public and threw a fit. We discussed dinner and concluded that none of us were hungry and we should wait until we got close to the hotel. About one minute after we decided this, Granddad starts pointing out places to eat. I say, are you hungry? He said, no, and I said, well, then let's just stick to the plan of waiting till we get back near the hotel to eat.

"Damnit, Landon, we are not eating at the hotel, Landon! It's too damn expensive, damnit."

Mother chimes in and I stop her, then I say, "Look, old man, you are misunderstanding me! When I say get back near the hotel, I mean that we need to get back close to the hotel, not eat there! Hell, I don't even think they have a restaurant open at night!"

"Oh yes, they do," he replied, and I said, "Well, we just need to find a place close to it as nobody's hungry yet."

Silence for about three minutes until he comes up with the best idea he had for all the road trip and said, I know, then he told my mother and she replied, "Daddy, it's closed down!"

His stubborn ass said no, it's not, and took us there, where we had the best BBQ in Virginia and I'll be damned if while we are eating a man next to us says, "You couldn't have been in WWII, you're too young." (He was referring to my granddad's hat and jacket that my sister and her husband had got him.) At first Granddad looked annoyed, and he said it again, and my granddad laughed.

Then the man said, "Roxcie?" She turned and looked at him, and my ears perked up like a Doberman. "You're just as beautiful as you have always been," he said. I was amazed that this random hole in the wall that she used to eat at when she was a teenager had a man that recognized her after fifty years! He was the owner, and they were cute, talking about their teenage years and catching up. Then my grandfather cockblocked them for a lack of words and said they had to go, it was getting late. I personally think he doesn't want her to meet anyone else as it would leave him alone, but that's just a guess.

My top three moments of the day: Number three, putting flowers on everyone's grave, even random strangers, referring to the old flowers that Granddad was going to throw away. When I did this, he said, what are you doing? I replied it's better than nothing at all, and he said, "I would rather have nothing at all than faded flowers."

I said, "Okay, I'll remember that when you are dead." Then I asked grandmother that if she was lonely that she could have him now—just joking.

Number two was meeting and talking with Cousin Tony, and number one was eating real BBQ with (mustard coleslaw! yummy) and having my mother reunite with a childhood friend! It was adorable and will probably make my top list for the whole trip!

My bottom three moments of the day: Number three, my grandfather saying, "See here, this was nigger town," followed by about a dozen more N-bombs in maybe less than a minute! I really hate that word, and it makes my skin crawl when he says it all the time, that and when he refers to them as colored people.

Number two was my grandfather throwing a fit at the cemetery and the bickering between him and my mother during what I thought was a special moment and the whole reason for the trip!

Number one was when I got upset with my mother for constantly defending me and trying to pamper him and repeating everything for him while we are talking. I got so upset and let her know why, but it just makes him happy to see me upset with her for defending me, if that makes any sense. I hate when he gets happy from her sadness. It's not right! I also hate making her sad, but she caters to his every need and never disagrees or argues with him, and she tries to smooth everything over, and I'm like, no Mom, I meant what I said, and I don't need you repeating everything he hears more than he lets on!

Believe it or not, this was actually a great day and probably the best day since day one. Mother seeing her old friend at the BBQ place pulled it up a lot ☺. I tried to get to bed early, taking three Tylenol Pms, as I have not slept good for the last three nights due to snoring coming from the old man, my mother, and Maggie, the dog, which may be the worst of the three. My grandfather is being considerate as my mother says repeatedly, "Turn it up, he can't hear it."

"Granddad, do you want me to turn it up?"

"No son, I'm fine."

Mother: "I know he can't hear that, turn it up for him."

"Granddad, can you hear it?"

"Yeah, I'm fine. I just want to see the weather."

Mama": "I know he can't hear that. Landon, turn it up for him."

Granddad: "What did they just say? Something about a fire and two dead."

That's when I say, "Fine, I'll turn it up." Now I can't sleep because I have a TV three feet away from me blaring at volume forty-three. My grandfather just wants to watch the weather, and my mother is just trying to please him, and I get no sleep, but I am fully expected to rise and shine at fracking 7 a.m.

Sunday:

WOW! What a day! This is going to sound a little crazy, and I half-way don't want to write it down because I see that it looks crazy. Last night around 4 a.m. I awoke suddenly and wide awake! (This after taking four Tylenol Pms and not getting to sleep until around 2 a.m. See Saturday for further details on that.) So I open my eyes and stare at the ceiling, and all I hear is snoring, and maybe it was the sleep aid, I don't know, but I swear I heard voices coming from my grandfather's snores, just like on *Ghost Hunters*! I really recall hearing "hello" over and over again, followed by me saying, "Hello, who is this?"

I could not make out the answer, so I asked, "Is it Grandma?"

And I heard a "no," so I asked if it was Grandma again? And I heard a distinct "No." I was like, who else could it be? Then I looked threw my photos and remembered who was on the graves we visited, and I said, "Mrs. Hinton?"

"No."

I thought, *Okay, maybe I'm crazy, it's just sounding that way.* I closed my eyes and tried to go back to sleep, and I swear instead of "no" I started hearing "Hello" again! I did the math in my head and realized that Mrs. Hinton was not my granddad's mother. Her death was in 1924, according to the pics, so I say, "Is this Granddad's mother?" And I get a vague "Yeah," followed by horse noises, like Mr. Ed. Yeah, I know it sounds nuts, but you kinda had to be there. I had a tough time figuring out what she was saying but heard the words "son" "grave" and "my flowers." This is crazy, because when I was at her grave earlier, I asked for her help with Granddad, which I also asked my grandmother ☺. As soon as my mother woke up, I said we have to go back to the graveyard, and she said okay. The day before, Granddad had insisted we put double flowers on her grave, and I had a strong suspicion that she wanted her flowers shared with her son who was shot to death by a clerk at the corner store in an accident, just months before she was murdered by her husband, and just before he committed suicide! I thought if it were me, I would have still have been mourning over him if I was her, and it makes sense in my head. I awoke at 8 a.m. Yeah, my granddad let me sleep in a little! I was flipping through channels when I heard a preacher talking about positive energy, and I listened, and he started talking about ignoring what other people say and think and turning away from negativity! I was like, *Look Mom, it's what I have been preaching to you, but it's actually a preacher! Listen to it!* I went and had breakfast, where Granddad and I cut up and had fun with the black waitress☒ Then I take Mother her breakfast and tell her Grandpa has signs of dementia. He had mentioned taking the OJ to her three times in a row and had no recollection of me telling him. He also did a few other things in a short period, and it reminded me of Mrs. Farrar, an Alzheimer's patient at LHV before she got bad.

I told Mother, who had started the morning arguing with him over the plans for the day as he had changed them. I told her about his disease, which she already knew about, and let her know that it eases up and crashes down at different times. He can go a week with no symptoms and then have a really bad few days with multiple symptoms and bursts of short-term memory loss, which is why he kept getting lost yesterday. I told her the worst thing she can do is to fight it and that she just needs to kinda roll with bounces and not stress or fight them if they are not game changers. She had argued with him about twenty-five times over us leaving Sunday instead of Monday, and this may be my fault as I told her I needed to get back and find a job, but I told her it is okay, we came all this way and might as well stay an extra day or two if we need to. She understood better how to cope and did fantastic, not arguing or pointing out his mistakes today! All that was doing was frustrating him and creating anger that he was slipping! WOW! Like a medical breakthrough, I felt like today we made the whole trip worthwhile! But wait! We're not done yet. If you get the breakthrough with Mother, today only, with the spirit's help, you get the breakthrough with Grandfather too! Yes, you heard me correct, Grandfather admits (with nothing manipulating him except his own brain) that he is slipping and losing his short-term memory! It totally made getting lost another six times, including three of them in a fort on a small island, worthwhile! For me it was not one but two medical breakthroughs in the same day! We talked for forty-five minutes about the disease and he said, "Yes, but others don't realize it. I do."

I said, "Grandfather, could you lift one hundred pounds when you were young?" He said yes. I said, "Can you lift thirty pounds now?" He said no. I said, "That's right, your muscles deteriorate as you get older, right?" He said yes, and I said, "Your brain is no different! But yes, at least you realize it, right!" And he was like, yeah, and I said there is no shame in asking for help after eighty-eight years, right, and he was like, no, I guess not.

Okay, so back to the spirits I encountered last night. I chatted with whom I believe to be my grandfather-in-law's mother last night.

And I figured out that she wanted me to share her flowers with her son.

So I go out to their graves with Granddad and with a plan to distract Granddad because I don't think he will be happy with removing the flowers, as he had demanded and argued we put double in front of her grave the previous day. When we get there, he goes down the wrong the road, parks, and I look and see an American flag on the road that is in good condition. (We removed a torn-up one from Granddad's middle brother the day before.)

I pick it up and we drive to the grave as granddad realizes he is a street over. When we get there I have my adrenaline up and I have Mom distract Grandfather long enough for me to take half of the flowers off of his mother's grave and onto her first son's grave. Well, I look out the window and say, "Mother, is that what I think it is?"

I hear, "Yes, son, it looks like some flowers came loose. Can you go put them back for us?"

Granddad says, "Impossible. I double checked them myself. We put them in good!"

I remember packing them myself and asking Granddad if he was satisfied and to double check. Also, if the storm blew them up, why would they be only a few feet away on the ground and not caught on the fence? I was super happy. I felt like I did a good deed for a spirit from another realm! I planted the flag, the rose I snagged from my grandmother's grave, and the bushel of yellow flowers that were laying on the ground mere feet away from the grave where they were to go. And as I left, I whispered, "Please help with Granddad. I love you, and may peace be with you."

Grandfather was nice all day long! We went to eat at Golden Corral, his favorite place, and it was packed wall to wall with black people, and I could tell it frustrated him, but he showed no anger and referred to them as black people all day! This is huge, as he has always bothered me calling them the N-word or colored in the past! Why the change today? Nah, it couldn't be, could it? Ah, it's probably coincidence. The sudden change in how he refers to black people, the sudden breakthrough with his memory lapse, the joking around and overall 180-degree change in attitude? I have a very scientific mind, and because of this I still have doubts. However, I do lean toward the fact that I was able to communicate with the spirit world. In my mind there is 95 percent that it was spirits and 5 percent chance it was all just coincidence! What a day. I loved it! Oh, and he took us down to Virginia Beach, and I remembered things from my childhood, like salt water taffy;

I got to see where my mother went to dance, and go on dates after high school;

I went to the boardwalk, where I remembered getting stung by jellyfish in the Atlantic Ocean and got my picture taken with Neptune. Yeah, I know, I need to hit the gym. We pulled up to the beach, and the birds took off and gave us a show;

I got to take a picture of my grandfather next to a WWII amphibious assault vehicle;

And my mother got to see her lighthouses ☺.

Not to mention seeing my Grandmother's grave look so pretty!

I'm euphoric right now! I am super stoked about the progress we have made, both physically (I told my mother I will keep working out and doing push-ups and chin-ups every day to be able to lift her up and around, if she will promise to keep working her leg to make it easier on me to lift her up), and mentally (for my grandfather understanding he has a disease and changing from angry and spiteful to cheery and thoughtful, and my mother, who was always the sunshine in my life and was almost broken by his mood swings and attitude actually bounce back and really being positive again). It's the first day of the trip that I can't wait to wake up in the morning!

I finish writing this and go upstairs right after the game ended, and my mother high-fives me as her underdogs beat the Patriots in the Super Bowl. I chat with my granddad, and he asks for something else on television, so I find *Law and Order* at 9:55, and it goes off. Then I go to CBS and find *NCIS*, my granddad's favorite show, and then five minutes pass and my mother says it's a repeat, so I go back up the channels to *Law and Order* again, and the first channel I find is local news at 10:07, and Mother says there, he wants to watch the news! I said okay and we started watching the news. I even joked with Granddad and said, well, we didn't get the pretty one tonight and noticed he had his eyes shut. Then a Navy story came on, and I said did that ever happen to you, Granddad? He did not reply and had his eyes shut. Then at 10:34 he gets up and says, "I have gas! I have to leave."

We say, just go to the bathroom. He says, "I have gas, Roxcie. I 'm going for a walk."

She says, "Daddy, why can't you just go to the bathroom?"

Then he told us, "I had to watch that damn baseball (meaning Super Bowl), and then I finally get to watch *Law and Order.*" He snatches the remote out of my hand and changes it! "I'm going for a walk, damnit!"

Then my mother does it. She argues and says, "Daddy, we were watching your news for twenty minutes now!"

He says, no, you weren't, and I try to explain to him what happened, and as soon as I say something, my mother says very loudly, "DADDY! We were watching your news!"

I say, "Mama, please! Be quiet. You're not helping."

He says again, "You snatched the remote and changed my *Law and Order*!

I said, "Granddad, you're wrong on this one."

Then again, "Daddy! We were watching the news! Daddy!"

He starts to walk out the door. "Daddy! Daddy!"

The door shuts and I start punching the mattress in a rage.

Everything I just wrote and felt is gone! I yell, "Mama, what is wrong with you? I thought you understood!"

She replies, "Well, I'm not going to let him hate on you because you were not wrong, son!"

I yell, "I know, but I can take it, damnit!" And I rage on the mattress again, showing my anger! "Mama, why do you argue? It makes things worse. Let me talk to him, damnit! Why, Mother, why do you insist on making me this angry?" When I said this she starts balling and crying and my rage turns to tears as I can't take seeing my mother in tears yet again! So much sadness! I quickly calm down and take the opportunity of him leaving to counsel her. I rush to find my laptop and boot it up to show her what I just wrote! Mama? Mama?

She replies, "Huh, huh, I. I am, I am so, I am so, so sorry," whimpering as tears roll down her face!

And I with tears rolling down take her hand and say, "Mama? Mama? Please calm down so you can hear me! You cannot argue, Mama! You wouldn't argue at JW, would you?" (JW is a mentally challenged boy from next door.) She replies no, whimpering, and I said of course not, he has a disease and you know that, right?

She whimpers. I say you can't argue! She replies with, "So I'm just supposed to let him be mean and hurtful when we have done nothing wrong?" I say, "Yes, Mama, he has a disease! Mrs. Farrar did the same thing. The people that take care of her and love her, she accuses of stealing and turns mean, but the next day she's back to being nice. I've seen it. I know how this disease works! Let me take the hits, and you sit quiet on the sideline, Mama! You are not strong enough. You make things worse!"

She has almost stopped crying and I have dried up. I ask her if she could go stay with my sister for a week or two to get some rest and relaxation. She says you want me gone? I say no, Mama, but I can deal with this and you can't. She says she doesn't understand the disease and I say, Mama, you need to relax. Please go, and she refuses. Then I start reading her what I wrote not but a few hours before, ecstatic at the success we had today, and Grandpa walks in the room, so I quit reading and ask her if she could read. She says yes and reads it. I ask him if he is okay. Yes, he replies, and I look at my mother and tear up and say, "Mother, I love you!" And I pack up my laptop to come downstairs and write.

Grandpa says, "Landon, you don't have to leave, please, I didn't—"

I interrupt him and say, "Granddad, I am not leaving because of you, buddy. My mind was tired, and it just woke up, I have to go write, that's all. It has nothing to do with you, buddy. I love you both, okay. I'll be back when I'm done writing, just like earlier, okay. We're going to have a great day tomorrow." I smile at him as I shut the door, then tear up as I enter the hall of the hotel. I come down to write this and as I try to put my emotions in check and quit crying, it's back upstairs. I hope they are sleeping, and I can get some sleep for the first time in a while. I just took three Tylenol Pms and will take some Xanax to get some sleep, as I fear now a long road trip home ☹.

The next morning things go relatively okay. We go to city hall so he can get the grave situation settled, and then we go to the grave. I call the city hall and the supervisor meets us at the grave site. He repeated the same thing three times to her in a row, and then I spoke with my mother about how he got upset earlier when she would ask, "Daddy, look, is that where we used to ...?"

He would reply in an angry voice, "I don't know, Roxcie! Damn school, hell if I know. I don't care."

I said to Mother to please talk to me and let him drive. She seemed perturbed, and I said, "Mother, I need you to remember these four numbers 3038, okay?" She went to write it down, and I said, no Mama, just remember them. Then I said, hey Mama, is that where you went to movies as a kid? Yes. Hey, is that where you ate? No. Hey, did you eat there? No, those are new, son. Hey mama, what was that number? Three, zero … ? I don't remember, and when we got to the grave and he went inside the office, I said I'll catch up. This gave me time to explain how the same way she couldn't remember the simple four-digit number is the same reason he gets all upset when you ask him questions while he tries to remember what he is doing. I would think Mama, that is why he repeats the same things over and over again, like yesterday when I counted that he told us why we were going in reverse of the way we should be going nine times in a two-hour period. When the normal person wants to remember they repeat the number or words over and over again in their head, right? Well, Granddad is a tough son of a gun, and he is fighting this disease the best he can! He doesn't want to forget, and he knows he is going to unless he keeps thinking about it, and this why he says the same thing over and over and why he gets mad when Mother or I would say you told us that three times already.

He yells, I know, damnit. I'm sorry, but I can't concentrate! It really is sad, looking back and that I was so upset at the way he was acting and that it took me so long to understand that he has this disease. I would have been a bit more understanding. However, he has done a very good job of hiding the fact that he is slowly slipping and losing his mind. My mother always says it's never his fault, he always has an excuse, and that's because he does not want anyone to know he is slipping. He also repeats the same stories over and over again, probably because they are the only ones he can still remember.

I also see that he will take something you say and say it a few minutes later, as if it was his mind that came up with it. My mother would get perturbed when he would do this and remind him of who just said the same thing. This often resulted in him getting angry and demanding we do something, as if to prove he is in charge. I will need to research this to see if this is a symptom, as I'm sure it is. I might say, "Hey, Granddad, how does BBQ sound?

A few minutes later I hear, "Hey, I know what we can eat! How does BBQ sound?"

My Mother would get upset and say, "Daddy, Landon just said that," and he would do this with almost everything. I remember Mother saying, "No, Daddy, James told you that," and so on. I wrote some of this as I waited at city hall, where my grandfather went to the mayor's office. The mayor's office was closed, so we went to the city manager's office, where Mr. Godfrey was nice enough to spend a few minutes to comfort an old vet.

Then we get in the car with Grandfather satisfied and we head back home. As I sit here typing this, he gets lost and we get him on the right path. He mentions something odd as he is driving and says, "Maybe I should move into the senior center."

Mama replies, "No Daddy, you never wanted to do that, remember?" and he replies, "Well, if something happened to you I would probably sell the house,"

I said, "You will always have me, Granddad." However this shows me that things are worse than I originally thought if a man who has always been anti-nursing home is now considering it! I'm scared because I know he belongs there soon, and I also know Mother loves him too much to put him there. However, I don't believe she knows just how bad this disease gets and that he can be a danger to himself and others if it gets to that point. Well, my battery is going to die, so I will have to write more later.

We just got to the hotel, and it was a decent day traveling, albeit short. I nodded off in the back seat because I was running on very low sleep. I awoke when he got upset that I was missing the beautiful countryside, and I appeased him by staying awake and chatting with him. We went to see his other grandmother's grave. We were trying to make it to Raleigh, and my grandfather wanted to have us eat at Gardners (famous for its BBQ buffet) and that's when we filled up on some really good Southern cuisine. We decided to make it to Raleigh, North Carolina, for our stopping point. He said,

"Look, the way I see it, if we get to Raleigh we can wake up and take our time instead of being rushed."

I replied, "Granddad, we have no schedule, right? Why would we be in hurry either place?"

This upset him, and he said, "Landon, I never said we had to hurry! Don't be saying I said that when I didn't!"

I said, "Yes, sir, I'm sorry."

No longer than five minutes later he decided to pull in to a motel. My mother politely said, "Daddy, I thought we were going to Raleigh?"

He replied with an angry voice, "Roxcie, leave me alone! I'm just checking these rooms, damnit!"

I looked at her and she left it alone. I'm thinking that he is upset that he cannot drive in the dark and is upset at my mother for emphasizing that fact. He later admitted that he changed his mind because it was getting dark. When we were going into the hotel, Mother said I need my black bag from the car, and he yelled, "Roxcie, we would have to unload the whole trunk to get to it. You don't really need it!"

I allowed this to upset me and opened the trunk and within three seconds retrieved everything we needed. I snapped at him and said, "Granddad, what if you were disabled? Would you want to be treated like that? No! You wouldn't, buddy, and don't try to say you would, because I know better."

This upset him, and I was fine with it, as I was fed up with him treating Mother like a dog! I take that back, because he actually treats Maggie, his dog, better than he does his own daughter! I have been full of sadness today as I realize I have a mother who is physically handicapped and a grandfather who is mentally handicapped and have basically lost a whole person. I sent a distress email to my sister:

To: Sis

Re: Need Help Desperately!

Sunday, February 5, 2012 10:58 PM

From:

Sister,

I try not to be a burden or ever ask you for favors, but I desperately need your help right now! Please consider taking Mother for a week, maybe two! Please, I'm not sure how the trip home will be, and maybe by the time we get there I may not need to ask of this imposition from you, but all I know is this, Mother is having trouble grasping the reality of what is going on with Granddad! She has been beaten and battered emotionally and needs some R&R away from him to recharge her strength and understanding. Please read what I have written and let me know any thoughts you may have as to a solution? If you believe me to be hurting instead of helping, let me know, as I have no outside looks at my actions! I know I am unorthodox, but I seem to be making progress, but this is only going to get worse, and I need Mama recharged for the long haul! I feel like I am in his head. I can see how his brain is working and feel sorry for him. I just need some one-on-one time, I think! Please read and forward to Miah, maybe, and I may be too emotionally in this to see something I may be doing wrong. I am 100 percent honest, and if you can take it, then see if Miah can? It is emotionally charged and graphic. I did not hold back. I wrote what I felt. I love you and understand either way. There are large gaps where pics should be, so be sure to scroll all the way if you read, okay? XOXXO

She fell silent and has not emailed back or texted me since! I sent her a text last night saying please read your email first thing in the morning. This is twice she ignored the struggles of Mother and left me to deal with the burden of misery alone.

I fear once again I am letting the negative forces of the universe overwhelm me and struggle to even get a little happiness out of the day, which 99 percent of the time comes from Mother being strong when I fall weak. She always has a smile when I need it the most. However, I have shed more tears in the last forty-eight hours than ever before, and the sadness is overwhelming me as I know we have a long road ahead of us. I fear I will never have a normal life and will be alone when I grow old, without children or a wife to help me should any of these issues befall me. I feel alone and wonder how Mother has had the strength the last four years to deal with it alone. I checked her phone text and call history today, and my sister called her once on December 29th and once in November, with a few texts mixed in. I realize all the weight now falls on me, and I am determined to do whatever it takes to stand strong and help the best I can.

My father ran away and turned his back on the family, and it feels like my sister is doing the same. (I can't say she turned her back like my father. It's more like turning a blind eye.) Whatever the case, I need to suck it up and quit with the self-pity shit before I am consumed with negativity again! I wish and pray to God that he can help me through these dark times and that I can get another day like Sunday, where it seemed normal for a brief period, and allow me back some of the positive energy I need to keep going strong. I never knew how weak I truly was until this road trip! I smoked a cigarette tonight, breaking my vow to God of forty days without vices, and I pray that will be the only one, as I was able to go eleven days with nothing extra and hope I can finish the next twenty-nine without another slip. It is hard to see any light at the end of the tunnel, but I will not leave Mother in the dark to travel it alone! I am going to go upstairs and take enough Tylenol Pm to put a horse to sleep and pray that tomorrow is a better day!

Well the eighth day of our journey starts off rough, as I could not get to sleep until 2 a.m. My mother awoke at 6:43 a.m. in extreme pain, and I look at the clock and know we have to be quiet so as not to awaken Grandfather. (If he awakes this close to seven, we will all have to get up.) Mother insists he said we do not have to leave until 9 a.m. I am afraid she does not understand that what he says and what he does are not running together in his mind anymore. It is very upsetting to see the agonizing pain my mother is suffering. She says she twisted something. I can see the pain in her face as she reacts to it. I tippy-toe quite as a mouse to my bag to get one of my pain pills and tippy-toe to the bathroom for some water and back to her. I lean over and whisper, "This is for the pain. It will take about thirty minutes to kick in, okay?"

She says thanks and I get back in bed as quietly as possible. Thinking that the twist must have occurred when she halfway fell last night and caught herself on the wall, she had yelled for my help, and when I got there she was slipping but trying to keep from falling any more. This fighting to fall must have twisted something in the lower part of her back. Either that, or me lifting her to the wheelchair did something. Exactly at 7:03 Granddad awoke and looked at the clock and started stomping around making as much noise as possible in an effort to wake us up. When he left, he slammed the door! My Mother says, "He's mad at something." We brainstorm why he could be mad. He asked last night if I wanted to drive through the mountains, and I said no, I prefer not to go through there again, as the first time I felt like we could die at any moment. This was my guess. Mother said it was because we didn't jump up, and I would have to agree with her. We got up and are ready to go by 8 a.m. to try to appease him, but it looks like another rough day is in store.

Well, it was a very rough morning as we spent over three hours looking for a family graveyard, and Grandfather was having a very hard time with his disease. Mother had to be the strong one, as I got very irritated with his behavior. On the way to Raleigh, North

Carolina, I tried to nod off to catch up on a little sleep, and he purposely hit the road ridges on the side of the highway three times in a row to wake me up. I know this because he giggled when I awoke. Mother said, what is funny about that? He replied, I just like the noise it makes, and looked at me in the rearview mirror. (Spiteful man, he is.) When we drove around in circles looking for the grave site he was determined to make excuses for everything, from why he was lost to why people were honking and why he had to slam on the brakes. He kept asking random strangers on the street if they knew where it was, even stopping in the middle of a two-lane street to converse with a lady and back up traffic. When horns started honking and I looked to see four cars behind us, I told him he needed to go. He got angry with me and said, "Damnit, Landon, I'm trying to find out where this place is for you!"

I said, "Granddad, you can't just stop in the middle of the street like this, it's blocking traffic."

He said, "They can go around. It's just one car, damnit." He even stopped when he saw a state trooper pulling someone over and flagged him down for directions. When that didn't work, he stopped a FedEx driver for directions. After two hours of seeing him frustrated (I was not helping him at this point because he had upset me), I looked up the address on Google and located the cemetery for him.

"Granddad, I found it, I have a map," I said as he was yelling at other drivers for honking as he was going five miles an hour in a 45 mph zone. He refused my help for another fifteen minutes as he was determined to find it and was about twelve miles away.

He finally said, "Okay Landon, we'll do it your way."

I told him where to go, and about a mile from the street we were supposed to turn on he said, "This isn't the right way. I know where it is," and turned around. I was extremely irritated, as was he, and he drove for another five minutes and threw a fit about how the street signs were different.

I said, "Granddad, I know where it is. Please let me drive."

He replied with, "You can't drive in this, Landon." Once again he was treating me like a mentally challenged person who didn't live in the city for twelve years! I was angry at this. (Imagine, you know where the place is, and you want to help, but are powerless as you see a man drive in circles for three hours.) Mother took my hand as she saw the anger in my eyes and calmed me down. The tides had turned, as I was the one weak, and my mother had the strength today.

We finally found it after he stopped and asked three more times. He got out and had the leash in his hand and set Maggie down, unleashed. Then he started walking with his hand held out as if he was walking the dog and walked to the grave. Mother yelled, "Where is Maggie? I looked and saw that he had no clue the dog wasn't on the leash and informed him.

He said, "What? Maggie! Maggie! Come over here! How did you get off the leash?" After we got back in the car and drove away, he felt better about himself. He then started reading signs out load, like "Hospital two miles," and then he would say, "Now, if my memory is correct there is a hospital up here." Then again, "State fairgrounds next left, there should be fairgrounds over this hill on the left."

Mother giggled and said, "You're just reading the signs, Daddy."

After we went by the few family markers we had on the agenda and got on a piece of highway that was straight until our stopping point, he finally let me drive. I was driving and had my left-turn signal on. I turned my head to see in the right mirror and he yells, "Damnit, Landon, I'm not trying to spy on you! Just leave me alone."

I said, "Grandfather, I just turned my head to see if the lane was clear. I'm not going to put up with these outbursts you're having! Your mind is playing tricks on you, and I had no thoughts of you spying until you just flew off the handle."

He said, "Well, yesterday you said that, didn't you?"

"Yes! Granddad, yesterday. I said that yesterday! Not today!"

Mother would take this little time I have to tell me stories of the good old days, which I really enjoyed hearing, and my jealous granddad would interrupt her every time by blurting out things like, "Forty-nine dollars Days Inn, what do you think about that?" and, "Free breakfast with stay."

 I know he did this intentionally, because I would say, "Granddad, that was rude. Mother was talking." Then he would let her finish. But as soon as she started another story he would do it again! I started hitting the brakes when he would do it from then on, and after the second brake check he quit and let us convers. I could see him in the back seat pouting, playing with Maggie, saying "Yes, you're a good girl. Daddy's little girl, you never argue with me or fight with me, you my baby. Yes you are."

After a good twenty minutes of silence, I felt sorry for him and decided to strike up a conversation. "Hey buddy, how far do you think we will go tomorrow?"

"Damnit, Landon, I don't know! You expect me to know everything! How the hell am I supposed to tell you that!"

I replied, "Listen, Granddad, I was just trying to make conversation with you. I said how far do you think? I was looking for an answer like Tennessee or maybe Alabama, not a precise location! Just trying to chat, but that is obviously not something I should do with you anymore, is it?"

He apologized, and, tell you the truth, the rest of the night was pretty good! He really had a pathetic episode as we were discussing the hotels. He kept forgetting and saying the same things over and over. I would say, "It's okay, buddy, we are almost there. Yeah, buddy, I know you told us. No, buddy, we already decided to go to this hotel on exit fifty-five."

He would say, "No, we did not!" and then a few minutes later, "You were right, I'm sorry."

I told Mother that when I saw he was struggling I would refer to him as "buddy" but when I thought he was just being grouchy and spiteful Grandpa (aka himself) I would say "Granddad." Mother was happy to finally start understanding what was going on and how to better deal with it. She has been better than me with being understanding the last few days. Still no word from my sister, so I sent her a quick text saying: Hey sis, disregard the last text and email, we are just peachy (sarcastic) I love ya and see ya on Mother's Day ☺.

We pulled into Ashville and checked into a motel. The nice little girl at the desk recommended a great place to eat called the Cornerstone. We got back to the motel, and a car was taking up two spots in front of our room. I was getting Mother in the room, and Grandpa said he was going to go park the car. After six or seven minutes passed I went to find him. He was knocking on everyone's door, asking them if that was their car. I said, "Granddad, you can't just wake everyone up because of one person's mistake."

He waived me off, so I went in and vented to Mother. Sure enough, he came in a few minutes later with a big smile on his face and said, "See, I did it!"

And I replied, "You sure did, buddy," then left to go write. I can't wait for another fun day.

Well, it was a good morning. I actually got six hours of sleep last night, a luxury for me. Last night we tried to get to sleep around 11 p m., and with all the lights and TV off there would be silence. Then about every three to five minutes until twelve fifteen, Granddad would say, "Landon?"

I would reply with a faint, "Yeah?"

"Would you like to drive when we get on the highway?"

"Yes, sir."

Then a few minutes later, "Roxcie?"

"Yes Daddy?"

Faintly followed by, "Would you like to go to Cherokee tomorrow and show Landon?" (something she has expressed about a dozen times previously). This went on for about an hour, even startling me at points. Mother says when I went to write last night he said lots of good things about me, including, "I'm not meaning to scream at him. I talk loud, but I really wasn't fussing at him," and how he was excited about the day's events.

This morning, he was bad, and he was forgetting a lot of things. He took Mama's coffee thermos to fill it up and was looking around the breakfast area frantically for it. I found it in the trunk of the car. He forgot his waffle and spilled his coffee all on the seat and himself. He tried to check out three times, and I had to help him like you would help a young child. He was definitely in buddy mode, as the disease had a grip on him strong. I really felt sorry for him, as did the lady at the desk, who talked to him and comforted him. He seems to be better now that we are on the road. He loves me and even though he can be very mean-spirited at times and does things that irritate the hell out of me, I love him with all my heart, too! I'm going to put this up now as we are sightseeing through the Smoky Mountains and it really is pretty. (He is actually going the speed limit and has only run off the road once. I must keep an eye out for our safety.)

Noon high, and we just stopped for a snack at Devil's Courthouse, peak elevation 5500. It has been a nice drive, and we got lots of pictures as Granddad has been very sweet, although Mother just told me that she told him I was writing a book about this trip last night, so this could explain his reversal in attitude. It has been beautiful. We encountered thirty minutes of light to moderate snow, and then it cleared up and the sun came out! He has only gone off the road four times and only crossed into oncoming traffic twice! He has been a joy to be with today, and my mother and I are having a nice time with him. I find the mountains to be peaceful and wish I had the time to hike some of it. He makes it seem like it's Mother's fault we can't go hiking because she is in a wheelchair, but I know he wouldn't go anyways, as he was scared to climb up a handful of steps earlier to get a picture with me.

WOW! What an incredibly great day! We drove through the Smoky Mountains and stopped at all the lookouts and took pictures. I felt like we were a normal family on a great family vacation for a change, until the car overheated and my grandfather's mood drastically changed! He got so upset, he could no longer enjoy anything. Everything my mother said after the car overheated was answered with, "I don't know, Roxcie. Damnit, quit talking to me. All I can think about is the damn car!" He was rude and mean-spirited again, all because the car overheated. However, if I said something he would be cordial and agree or disagree but see my side. When we got to Cherokee he pulled over and opened the coolant and filled it with water and then took out the water for fear of overfilling when he read the cap. Then he checked the oil. When he finished he put the oil dipstick into the coolant. I yelled, "No, buddy, that's the coolant. Don't put that there!"

He said, "I know that, Landon. I was just checking the coolant level." I don't think he was checking the coolant, as it was transparent, and he was pushing it in and twisting. Then he got in the car, then got out of the car, then filled the coolant again to the top and then drained it and we left. A few miles down the road he stopped, got out, and tried to fill the coolant again. I felt so bad for him as he told us what he thought the issue was at least twelve times in a row, as if he was trying to memorize again. I really feel that is what he may have to do these days, as he knows his mind will forget. I tried to get Mother to not say or do anything for the duration of the drive in an effort to keep from upsetting him. It was a long drive to the next town as we went forty-five mph the whole way.

We were on an Indian settlement, and it was not ideal to have a broken-down car. I tried to get him to pull over when the car maxed out at hot and shut down the AC and was flashing OVERHEATED on the dash. He thanked me for my concern, but said he knew what he was doing. The car was not leaking fluid, just overheating, but by the time we got to the hotel it was leaking fluid. I'm afraid he may have made a three-hundred-dollar problem into a thousand-dollar problem. I told him we needed to find a place to stay and go eat as Mother and I were starving. He agreed, even though he said he wasn't hungry, as the only thing he could think about was the car. We got to the restaurant and he ate a salad and chicken fried steak. My Mother had half of her BLT and a few onion rings. I tried to get her to eat more and told her she could not live on what she ate. My food (crab-stuffed tilapia) was forgotten by the waitress, and I settled for just the salad bar this evening.

Why, you may ask? Well, let me explain for you. Halfway through dinner, my grandfather asked me a question, and my mother could not hear. She asked him to speak up, and he replied, "I just don't get it, Roxcie! If I speak up, I'm yelling, if I don't, you jump on me for not talking! Son of a bitch!"

She replied to me, "Here we go again."

They started bickering, and I said, "Really? We are going to ruin a great day and cause a scene in public?" I felt like my father did when my sister and I were young, like I was dealing with two small children who would not stop misbehaving. My grandfather put his hands over his eyes and stared straight down at the table. When I told him to not do that, he replied, "I'm just resting my eyes," in the same way he did when he was pouting the day he got upset and lost thirty minutes in Virginia. I was in awe at the anger I saw in both of them☒ I walked off, and, yes, I broke my promise to God and had another smoke to ease the emotions I was feeling. It is a lot to deal with, and I see the fact that if I was not in the picture their arguments would be shorter and less heated. When it was just the two of them, that's all they had. They had to make up and play nice; there was no Landon, no other option.

I went back to the hotel room after the arguing had stopped and talked to them about tonight. My grandfather's way of handling things was, "Landon, I can't live this way. I'm going to rent you and your mama a car and let y'all go on home, and I'm going to take my car and you won't have to worry about me anymore! I just can't live this way."

I could tell he was playing the sympathy card, and if I knew for 100 percent that I was talking to Grandfather and not "Buddy," I would have called his bluff. I could not be certain that he would not commit suicide, so I talked them through the argument. I got Granddad to admit he had treated Mother very disrespectfully today. I also (although much harder) got my mother to admit she may have let the constant abuse to manipulate her mind into thinking he was being mean when maybe he wasn't. Although I believe there was an 85 percent probability of his intentions being out of spite, I wanted to show her there was a chance she was wrong. It was not until she admitted she could be wrong that the issue actually got resolved. They both thanked me as I left to type this, although I could sense a bit of gloating in my granddad's tone.

When I get back to the room to go to bed, they are still jabbing at each other quietly and only to me. I get to the room, and he whispers to me, "Landon, we may have a serious problem with the car."

Mother whispers, "He's milking it," and back and forth we go again. My Mother goes to the bathroom, and he talks to me, trying to manipulate me into thinking he's the good guy and get sympathy votes. I tell him he's just as much at fault as she is, and he doesn't need to be so rude and sharp to her when he gets upset. I tell him that every time something upsets him, he takes it out on her verbally, and he goes into super whisper mode, "I know, I know, I do that. I need not to." It's this super whisper that proves to me this is a game to him. He doesn't want her to know because it gives her case more ammo.

I pretend not to hear him as he chats with me because I'm tired and want to go to sleep. At 1:44 a.m. I awake to hear my mother struggling to get up. I rush to help her and ask if she needs to go to the bathroom. She replies, "No, I just need my medicine."

I ask her if I can just go get it for her, and she replies that I can't as I don't know where it is. I try to help her up, and after a few minutes of struggling tell her it's a tiny motel room; it can't be that hard to find, just let me get it for you. She refuses, and this hurts me tremendously, that my own mother doesn't trust me! She must think he has manipulated me and that I'm capable of throwing away her medicine. He repeated many times earlier that it must be the medicine she takes that is making her this way. Completely hurt, I become wide awake and start typing again. How can my own mother think such thoughts of me, that I would do such a thing? I am hurt by this deeply and now will have to turn my back on my grandfather in order to prove to my mother that she can trust me. It was not until a few years later that I would find out my mother had a raging addiction to painkillers, and that I would take away the excess, giving her assumption truth.

I woke up this morning in hell. He was up at 6:45 a.m. and eating breakfast at 7. I woke up and got dressed to go eat with him. I talked to him, and he asked me to stay with my mother while he took the car into the shop. He wanted me to talk to her and figure out how to make things better. I decided that was a great idea, to try to get my mother on the right track, instead of wasting time in a service shop waiting room with a grumpy grandfather.

I talked to my mother, who went on about how my father turned on her and now her father is turning on her and how weak she feels. I explain to her that she feels weak because she does not eat or exercise. I spoon feed her yogurt as if she were a baby. She starts crying, and I talk to her about being negative, and she tells me that she is overwhelmed and has been backed in a corner too long. I try to tell her that every major religion refers to God being within and that she is not going to just wake up and be walking miraculously one day. That if she wants the Lord to help her, she needs to start from within. She finally tells me when this started with her and that it happened on her birthday the past year. My sister had planned a nice trip for them to stay with her in Abilene, but my granddad at the last minute backed out with the excuse of it costing forty-five dollars in gas to go. She said she would pay for the gas, and then he told her that he could not stand my sister Lachelle. Like any mother would do, she protected her young and defended my materialistic, selfish sister. This was the day after eighteen years that my mother stood up to him! Don't get me wrong, she still pampers him 24/7, but from that day on when he pushed too much she would fight back, as we saw last night. I asked her why she didn't say this last night, when he was pushing the fact that she had been acting this way for six months because of her medication. She replied with, "I just didn't think about it."

I find this hard to believe. We continue talking, and she tells me how hard it's been for her. She starts crying and saying how it's all her fault and that she has upset me and Grandfather and she needs to just stay quiet. I told her staying quiet is what leads to her losing control and that's the worst thing she could do. It does not solve anything. She says no, and I start using harsh language to get the point across. She starts crying more heavily and telling me a story about my sperm donor and so on. She wants to get up, so I go help her and she falls back down, crying as hard as she can. "Mother, what's wrong with you?"

She replies with how she can't take this, and how I am all she has and she is losing me. I get super angry and punch the wall, bloodying up my knuckles, then I go flip over the other mattress in an uncontrolled rage. She starts yelling how she is sorry and will not tell me anymore stories. This just fuels my rage as she completely does not understand why I am upset. I lay on the floor, balling my eyes out like a child, saying how I can't take this anymore and how I despise my sister for always leaving this on my hands and being able to escape it, how hard it is on me to deal with all of it on my own! How I wish I could just leave this world and start anew.

I cried until there were no more tears to fall. I explained to my mother that the only thing that makes me cry is seeing her cry, and that her stories don't phase me. It's her sadness or the thought of losing her that drives me insane and brings the sadness deep enough to cause a thousand tears.

About ten minutes later Grandfather comes back. It is 9:39 a.m. and he is smiling. "They say the car is okay. They couldn't find anything wrong, and it is running good. What happened to the mattress?"

I wanted to block the room off, I say, as it's none of his damn business. He asks why we are not ready and tells my mother to hurry up. He leaves the door wide open, with cold air gushing in. Mother ask him to close it, and he ignores her. He tells me to start packing up, and without being able to transfer my rage to paper yet he caught me at the wrong damn moment!

I yelled, "Granddad! You should be happy that we are not stuck here for three more days! Mother will take her time, so quit rushing her! She is crippled, and you said they might not even be able to look at it today! You should be happy, old man! Give her time and close the damn door. Can't you see she is cold and is not fully dressed! Be considerate, for once in your fucking life!"

What a day! Grandfather was livid when we were driving down the road, and so was I! We kept bickering back and forth, and I told him and my mother, "How about we play the quite game?" The best idea I could have had; why didn't I think about this earlier? It was so peaceful, he didn't say a word for like five hours! I read some of the Quran and was able to calm down and find peace. He did great except for when my mother asked him if he needed help when he was taking his jacket off. He jerked away from her and then slung the jacket into the back seat, smacking her in the face with it accidently, I think. He drove fast and furious for the first two hours, and I mentioned that all those years of watching NASCAR paid off! He actually drove decently, only hitting the sides when he wanted to wake me up. I then put on his heavy-duty sunglasses, and he could not see my eyes. I also asked him if he was going to keep up the hateful attitude. He did not say anything and pouted the rest of the way.

My mother and I were very sweet to each other and him, frequently asking him if he would like a drink or needed anything. Mother asked if she could turn on the air conditioning, and he did not answer, then turned it off right away. I said, "Mother are you hot?" She said she was, and since her window was broken, I rolled mine down and let the car cool down. About ten minutes later he turned on the air conditioning and seemed to be okay for a bit.

I would make comments like, "Wow, we have gone two hours without a negative comment," and "Mother, I think I'm getting my positive energy back." I could not understand how he always thought negatively. Even when the mechanic said the car was not broken, he had gone straight to thinking, well, we still lost a day! Un-freaking-believable!

When we got to Mississippi, he pulled over to get gas and broke his silence. He proceeded to explain his morning events right up to the point where he came into the hotel room and started being mean. He sounded like he had gone into Buddy mode, and I let it go, even though my mother and I noticed about five holes in his story. I told her I knew and asked her to let it go. Then we went and ate at Ryan's buffet, where he acted like a child who had just got into trouble and refused to eat much. We were like, suit yourself, Buddy. I was just concerned with my mother eating, and she ate well. When I got in the car I was waiving at Maggie, and he covered her with his arm and pulled her toward him, as if to say she's my dog. He powered through to Louisiana, where we stayed for the night. When pulling into the motel he slowed down with a car coming about fifty mph at my mother's side, and I yelled, "Mother, brace for impact!" Thank God the car slammed its brakes. Granddad went into the parking lot and said, "Ha, I got you on that one, huh?"

I said, "What! You almost killed us! You think that's funny?"

He said, "What? I didn't hit the dip!"

I don't know if he was in retarded buddy mode or had a suicide wish and wanted to take us with him, but I made my mother promise not to drive with him again. He says we should make it home tomorrow, and I will be in God's debt forever if we make it home safe! I told the man upstairs that I am buying a pack of smokes to help with my temper and anxiety as I powered through my Xanax at an astonishing rate and ran out two nights ago. I have still refrained from sex, eating junk food, candy, alcohol, and my desperately needed weed (for medical purposes, of course). I have realized one thing on this trip, and that is I am desperately needed, even if I have to sacrifice my life for a while to help my mother get better. There is not a doubt in my mind that she would not make it to seventy without my help. This is unacceptable. Since my grandmother Mitch died, she is all I have left in this world. I also believe with my sister shunning us and my grandfather treating her like dirt, I am all she has.

LAST DAY!

Well, I drove the whole way home because the last time I was in the car with him driving we should have died. It started off with a good breakfast and Granddad taking the motel for everything they had, leaving only one yogurt for any other guest. We had a good day and stopped by his favorite truck stop for a very good buffet. Mother slept a lot, and the old man and I talked for a long trip home. It was a great day until we got to Benbrook, Texas, and he told me we should stop by Wal-Mart in Granbury and get gas on the way home. He then said we would go by Stephenville and get Mother her hair dyed at Sally's and get some groceries. He explained the gas about two more times, and I said I know exactly where you want to get it.

He said, "Yeah, at the place right next to Wal-Mart. Should we go to Sally's first to get your Mothers hair dyed first? It is getting late."

I responded with, "So you want to get gas in Stephenville?"

Well, this angered him, and he snapped, "What? I told you we are getting gas in Granbury!"

"Yes, I know, but you said you wanted to go to Sally's first, right?"

He replied, "Yes, it's getting late."

I said, "So you want to gas in Stephenville?"

He yelled, "Landon, I told you, Granbury! I don't know why it won't sink in!" Then he explained where. Mother jumped in to my defense again, and here we go!

"Daddy, why are you yelling, he understands."

"Roxcie, why do you always have to jump in when we are talking, damnit! I am talking to Landon. Shut up!"

"Granddad, don't speak to her like that! Mother, why do you insist on?"

"Well, I can't help it. He shouldn't talk to you like that!"

"I can handle it, Mother!"

"Look, Landon. I'm going to tell you one more time, and hopefully it will sink in this time!"

"Granddad, I know what you are saying!"

"Well, obviously you don't, because you keep saying Stephenville."

"Look, Granddad, you said you wanted to go by Sally's first, right?"

"Yes"

"Then that means gas in Stephenville?"

Well, he blew up when I said this, and I found it somewhat humorous, but my mother got upset and I told them to not ruin a good day and drop it! We will get gas in Granbury. When we got there he pointed to the gas station, and I said it was fifteen cents cheaper at Wal-Mart, and he agreed to go there.

We saw a Sally's in the parking lot and I said, "Look, how about that? You want me to go in and get your stuff?"

Everyone agreed this was a good idea, so in I went. When I came out the two of them were screaming at the top of their voices! I got in the car and told them to quit! They calmed down, and my grandfather asked if she should be getting involved. I said no, she shouldn't, and he leaned back with his smug look (like HA! Told you so!).

I asked who brought it up anyways. He said he did, and I politely said, "Well then, Granddad, you were wrong for doing that, as we had agreed not to ruin a good day by arguing over petty stuff."

He was all like, "Well, if she hadn't had stuck her nose where it didn't belong."

I said, "How is this her fault? She defended her son, just like she would you or Lachelle! You are the one that won't let this go and are hell-bent on ruining a good day over a petty miscommunication!"

He said like he always does, "Okay Landon, that's enough, let's drop it."

I said, "Okay, dropped!"

Two minutes later he says, "Landon, I'm not dumb! I know what—"

I interrupted him and said, "I thought we dropped it?"

He said, "Well, I want to get this out!"

I listened to him explain this again and I started telling why I was confused and he interrupted me and said that's enough! We fell silent on the way to Stephenville and when we got to Wal-Mart to get milk and bread like he wanted, well, he said in his pouting way, "Roxcie can get in her buggy and go get it!"

I said. "NO! My crippled mother is not going in for milk and bread, you are! Quit acting like a three-year-old and go do what you were going to do before you got upset!" Why didn't I go get it, you may ask? Because he has tried this as punishment before, where if he doesn't get his way or is in an argument he punishes everyone else by refusing to do something or buy something. He is a jerk, and if I'm going to live with him, he is going to give up this behavior. I told him on the way home that if he wants a friend I will be a great friend to him, but if he wants a slave, I will stay for my mother, but I won't be a friend. A friend is give and take, and a slave is just give.

Three thousand six hundred and eighty-seven miles later we arrived home. We never once turned on the radio, and I learned a lot about my grandfather I would have rather not known. I rekindled my closeness with my mother and resentment with my sister. I got to see what a great vacation could be like and how a miserable vacation feels like!

Well, it's been a week since we've been on our road trip, and it is nice to be able to take a drive in town and get away, even if it is only for a few hours. I haven't written much because I've been busy looking for a job, rehabilitating my mother and making sure she eats right, and, you guessed it, struggling with my grandfather. The week had its ups and downs with my granddad. He forgot to lock the doors to the house, shed, trailer, and all within a week. This is something he has failed to do maybe three times in the eighteen years my mother has lived here. This shows me that the disease is getting worse. I have seen more of his mean streak in his attempts to spite me. Things were going okay for the first few days back. I swore never to let me or my mother ride with him again, but my mother made me when she had a doctor appointment and he was driving no matter what. Again it was a scary ride as he crossed into oncoming traffic multiple times, hit two or three curbs, and raced through a crowded Walgreens parking lot. I told my mother this is how she could lose the farm, in a lawsuit!

I can't quit smoking as he upsets me constantly. My mother, bless her heart, is trying really hard to keep me positive, but his constant negative energy is overwhelming at times. The week's climax was when we were cutting wood out back and the wedge I was using to split would bounce back up to fifteen feet at one point! Because of the danger to him, I would wait until he was out of range to split logs. I would go over and do pull ups on the tree limbs while I waited for him to get done cutting near me. He picked up the sledgehammer (the doctor told him not to lift anything above his heart, much less a sledgehammer) and went to split a piece of wood.

I yelled, "Wait, Granddad, that's my job!"

He said, "I just want to see if it will split."

I said, "We could see just fine if I do it."

He said, "Leave me alone, Landon. I'm going to see if it splits," and he raised the sledgehammer. I backed up and asked why he was being this way and told him I liked splitting the wood.

He yelled, "Well, you're not doing a damn thing, Landon! You're just standing there, so I'll do it my damn self. I don't need your help!"

I snapped, just lost control of my temper, and yelled back, "Why are you such a fucking jerk!?" and walked away in anger, leaving him alone.

He stomped around being angry all day, and I told my mother what happened. We sat inside and talked about how miserable and mean he can be. When he came inside after a few hours, I asked him (smiling), as I was in a good mood now thanks to my mother, "Granddad, are you okay?"

He started yelling, "My own children never talked to me that way, and I'll be damned if you are! Son of a bitch called me dirt trash. I've never been talked to that way, and I'll be damned if I'm going to now!"

I was in awe! Dirt Trash? How did he get dirt trash out of fucking jerk? I said, "I never called you that. I called you a jerk, not dirt trash!" I couldn't understand how dirt trash was worse than jerk anyways. This must be his mind playing a trick on him, maybe something someone said to him when he was younger. I don't know, but he sure did get mean! He started telling me how much everything I was drinking and eating cost, so I just started drinking water. He would wash dishes and set the table, but all my utensils would be dirty, not even rinsed. This just humored me, and I switched them to his place setting. He never washed them well anyways, so I always checked. The positive was he was super nice to Mother, and I'll take that trade any day! It's as if he knows he needs a friend and has to have one of us like him or be alone. If this is the case, I will take my mother's happiness over mine any day.

He got into a routine of having pouting time. (He would go to his room between four and five to make a point that he was mad.) Mother and I used this time to watch a movie and enjoy life. It was nice not having negative energy around. I would go by his room and say, "What a nice night, I sure wish Granddad could have been there."

He went on with his spiteful ways, and Mother and I went on smiling. I told him I liked what she was going to make for lunch and he turned up the stove twice to high, trying to burn it! I called him out on it and asked why he did that?

He said, "Oh, I thought I turned it down to low."

I told him how good the chicken and rice my mother made was, and he told her how awful it was, convincing her to throw it out! This upset me as I was hardly eating anything, so he could not use its cost against me, and they threw away four meals of food to the cats.

My mother begged me not to leave her, and I replied, "Mother, he can kick me out, and I'm okay with it! I will never leave you, though. I will set up a tent in the back if I have to, but I will never leave you again. I swear this!" I told her that he was a control freak and that he cannot control anyone but her. The only reason he can control her is because she lets him. He thrives off of it, so mean and controlling, so jealous and spiteful! Anything she likes or enjoys he takes away. He restates over and over again that he is the reason she is able to do whatever it is! He does this to the point it is no longer enjoyable, from taking a trip, to something as simple as drinking some orange juice. My mother and I were watching a movie on a rainy day, and he starts hammering on stuff right behind her, very loud!

I said, "What ya doing?"

He said, "Oh this door needs to be fixed!"

I laughed and winked at my mother. When he left I noted that he is like a five-year-old starving for attention and can't take the fact we control our own happiness, not him! He talks about everyone behind their back: Lachelle, James, Janey (my mother's only real friend in Blanket, Texas), my mother, and I'm sure myself. I often wonder if he is ever genuinely happy. I think he has not laughed or smiled genuinely since the '80s! I really feel sorry for someone whose only enjoyment seems to come from being mean. He would lock me out of the house and try to show his dominance on everything. If I did something, it was the wrong way, from putting too much ice in his tea, to the way I wash dishes, to how long I let Maggie out for. It was laughable but taxing on me. My sister came by for a "charity" visit on Friday. She said she would be there at 11 a.m., then called and said between two and three, and then showed up at 4 p.m. I wasted a whole day that I should have been out looking for a job! She finally showed at 3:56 p.m., and I stayed in my room. (I did not want to be upset and ruin my mother's enjoyment with her.) She left at 5 p.m., staying barely over an hour. I can't really blame her, as I did the same thing when I was distracted by the materialistic world. I can blame her for not caring or providing emotional support in a time her mother needs her the most! Her husband, Jerimiah, seems to be a hell of a lot more supportive and caring than she has ever been!

Still, I am afraid they don't see the gravity of the situation and how bad his mood swings get. I told my mother to pray for positive energy to fill the house, but I fear it will not happen until this mean old man is gone. After seeing his cousin Tommy, I fear it may be another five to fifteen years of hell! However, after seeing this disease progress as fast as it is progressing, I feel he has maybe only a few years left. I pray with all my heart that he can turn positive before his death, as I would feel no sorrow for the man as it stands today.☹

I see that this man is a total control freak! I helped Mother clean her room today and asked questions about peculiar things. She opened my eyes to a world very similar to that of the Jews in WWII. I asked why she had nine pairs of scissors in her jewelry box. She would not tell me in fear that he could be listening. A few hours later I shut her door as it intrigued me, especially after the fear I saw in her eyes. I asked her to tell me, and, in a whisper, she told me of how he would take them and tell her he didn't know what she was talking about and that it must have been Rachelle (my sister-in-law and someone at the time he didn't like). Then she told me about how he looked through her trash before he burned it. This is something I have seen him do in the short time I have been here. I just thought he was slowly putting it in; it did not register to me that he was monitoring the trash. Then I tried to clean the corner of her room, and she said not to touch it as she was blocking the door to keep her jewelry safe! I said, really? She replied he goes through everything! I asked how often, and she said very often! She told me numerous stories of how things Lachelle or I would give her would disappear or at the minimum be rearranged where he had gone through them. I cannot believe I let her live in this environment for so long and was clueless to how she had been made to live!

When I got done and walked out, he called me in his room and told me to shut the door (The first time he had ever done that). Then he proceeded to tell me that I needed to get on my knees to use his bathroom so I didn't piss on the carpet. This is something he had already mentioned to Mother, and there was no secret, so I know he told me to shut the door to get back at my mother! I laughed and apologized. I told him I would get down on my knees to take a leak and I would just use the toilet in the back of the house. Later that night, he saw my mother eating the yogurt, which I bought her to help maintain her protein level to rebuild her muscles, and he told us that he had bought sandwich meat for her to do that. We said how thoughtful, knowing that he just has to be the alpha male in control and has to top anything I do. I could care less, as it benefitted my mother, and told him that was thoughtful to get him gone. He interrupted our movie four times in the first hour, then, when I went to check on him, he asked how long movies usually last. I told him anywhere from eighty minutes to two hours usually.

He said it had been two hours already

I laughed and said politely that we had to pause it four times when he came in, remember?

He said, "Oh."

Later that evening, he called to Roxcie as he heard her coming down the hall. A few seconds later, she said, "Yes Daddy," and he replied, "Never mind, I forgot what I was going to say." This worried her tremendously, as it was such a short time.

The next day I dusted and vacuumed my mother's room for her, and then we worked out. She struggled, and I think she is just weak from the hard workout a few days ago (at least that's my hope). I am not so sure anymore that it is nerve entrapment, as her right arm being so weak also would point to a ministroke or another disease. I'm fifty-fifty, but in either case I feel with rehab and positive energy she can bounce back. Later on that day, her friend Janie came over to discuss the Bible.

Granddad had just come in from the yard, and I walked in and said, "What ya been doing?"

He replied, "Now that's a stupid question, Landon."

I said, "Yeah, you're right. My psychic abilities are failing me today!"

I went in and put the taco soup on the stove (about forty-five seconds), and when I got back the screen door was shutting. I asked Mother if I had upset him. She said, "I don't know, maybe you should check on him."

I waited ten minutes and went outside and asked if I upset him. He replied, "No, your damn mother told me to go outside, and I had just gone in! Janie comes over, and I have to leave, it's just not right, damn it!"

I said that's not right and started to walk inside, and he yelled, "Don't go tell her, Landon! Just leave it alone!"

I was upset and said okay and took a walk to have a smoke. I called Mother and asked her if she had said that. She said no, and then she asked Janie, and I could hear her say no also. He spent the rest of the day in his now normal negative pouting mood. Dinner was on at 2:45 p.m., and Mother rang the bell for him to come in; he did not.

I went out and told him, "Hey, buddy, we got dinner ready. It's really good, are you coming in?"

He replied, "I'm not hungry, Landon. Y'all go on and eat. It's soup, I can warm it up later.

I said, "You don't want to eat with your family?"

He replied, "I'm not hungry."

I said, "Suit yourself, buddy," and went in and ate. I left his salad, soup, and tea sitting in his place as we fixed it to remind him. He never touched it. He came inside went to his room and pretended to sleep. We could hear him creeping in the shadows but decided to enjoy ourselves instead of letting his negative energy bring us down. I cleaned the gutters and washed the dishes but left his meal just sitting there.

I asked him if he would like to watch the movie with us and he replied in a rude tone, "I'm watching *Wheel of Fortune.*"

I said again, "Suit yourself, buddy."

We left him alone and his meal still sat on the table where we placed it at 2:45. It is now 9 p.m. I refuse to allow Mother to be brought down by his negative energy and just try to stay upbeat and friendly in hopes he will see how happy we are and try to join in. However, I know he will never change, and I am truly saddened that he is incapable of being happy,☹

The next day was no better, as he kept his hunger strike going. I tried to talk him into coming for dinner, and he refused. I asked why, and he replied that he just can't do a damn thing right! I said what do you mean? He said that Roxcie yells at him every time he opens his mouth, so he's just not going to open his mouth anymore.

I asked him what she said recently to upset him, and he could not tell me, he only said, "Well, you saw it on the trip." I said I thought we put that behind us. He said, "I'm not talking about this anymore!"

I said, "Well, she had to do something recently, right?"

He said that when he talked about what we were supposed to work on in the yard, she started telling him everything I had done, and then he said, "I know what you do, Landon! I don't need her to lecture me."

I said, "Well, that couldn't have been all of it, what else has she done?"

He said he wasn't going to talk about it anymore. We ate dinner again without him, and when he finally came in I went to his room and told him he needed to eat.

He played the pity card and said, "Well, it's a good way to go, isn't it?

I said, "Why do you want to die?"

He said, "I have nothing to live for. I'm not going to live like this!"

I said, "You have a family, Granddad, that's worth living for, right?"

He did not reply.

I said it three more times. "You have a family that loves you and needs you," and then I left him alone. I went out back to think about what I could do and saw that he had taken all of the pretty silk flowers from the yard and put them in the fire barrel to be burned! This greatly saddened me, as it is one thing that brings joy to my mother. Later that day, James came over, and Granddad came out to visit, and it was nice. As soon as James left, he went right back to his room to mope. I don't think his mind is working right, and I'm at a loss to know how to fix it. It was nice when James bought his two granddaughters over, as it actually bought a little joy and happiness into an otherwise sad home.

When he was upset the other day, he mentioned that my mother had to go everywhere he went, and that he was a big boy and could go on his own. He doesn't need her to ride with him and she needs to stop!

I said, "Granddad, you don't have to worry about that anymore. I have talked to her because I was scared for her safety, so she won't be asking to ride with you anymore."

He said, "That's enough, Landon. I'm done!"

We didn't speak for a day, even though I would ask him if he wanted things or would play nice, but there was no breaking his mean streak. Last night I told my mother we were going to overwhelm him with positive energy! I made signs and put them up in every fridge and near his seat and wrote them in chalk on the sidewalk for when he steps outside. "You are loved, Granddad," "We love you so much."

I got up at 11:28 p.m. because I was hungry and couldn't sleep. When I went to the kitchen, I saw the living room fridge open, and as I turned on the water to rinse my glass he heard me shut the fridge and hid between the stove and the chair. To call him out, I walked in and turned the television on and looked at him.

I said, "Hey, Granddad, good to see you finally eating!"

"It's just a sandwich," he replied.

I said, "I'm a little hungry myself and I'm going to warm up some of this wonderful vegetable soup Mom made. Can I warm you up a bowl?

He said, "I don't want the damn soup! Y'all eat it all." He went to his room and shut his door.

The next day I was working Mother out, and he came in, rolled the wheelchair in the middle of the floor, and said "Y'all won't ride in my car, and y'all won't use it."

Well, we finally figured out that the only thing that is bothering him now is that I told him I was scared for Mother's safety when he drove. The next night he got into a knock-down, drag-out with my mother as I was away for a few minutes. He took the opportunity to go into my mother's room and tell her, "Can't you see, he's trying to control you?"

This set my mother off like a firecracker, even after the many times I have begged her to not let him bait her into an argument. When I went in to break things up, I simply asked why he did this.

"Stay out of it, Landon!" He started yelling at me and pointing his finger an inch from my face, and my mother started yelling even harder, hitting her head on the bar beside her bed. He was yelling for me to leave the house and that he doesn't want me here! I asked him why he hated me so much. And he yelled some more and slammed his door. I calmed my mother down after about forty-five minutes and told her to fight evil with good and shower him with love. He has controlled where and when she went, her finances, allowing her only $100 of her $600 Social Security a month. He has controlled what she did, what she ate, and monitored all phone calls and visitors, not even allowing her a phone in her room. He has truly controlled her for a long time, and complete and total control at that! The following morning my mother did as I instructed and was nice to him, and I came in to hear them having a nice conversation and waited for an entry point to play bad cop as my mother was playing good cop.

He said, "I'll be nice, Roxcie, I'm sorry. But he won't drive or ride in my car again!"

I said, "Every morning I start off with negative energy because of you! And why? Because I voiced an opinion that you didn't like?"

He said, "That's enough, Landon, stay out of this!"

I said, "Why? Because you said your side and that's the law? Yes, master! Whatever you say, master! You are the one that has controlled my mother and almost killed her! I have got her eating right, not worried about how much she is eating! I have her exercising and getting better, providing her with her positive energy and breathing life back into her! You're the one that makes her feel guilty and is a constant, controlling negative force! You're the reason for all your sadness, not me! You dwell on negative energy, Granddad, and you're jealous that we are having a nice time without you, as you sit on the outside looking in with hate and anger inside you! We want you to be happy and join us, but you refuse to!"

Well that was the gist of it. He interrupted me a lot when I was getting it out. Later that day he refused to eat with us, and then went in his room and ate and acted sick to get my mother's sympathy. She checked on him but managed to have a good time with me watching the *Lion King* for the first time. This was her fifth movie in the last eighteen years. He doesn't like watching movies, and so she doesn't get to watch them!

I put a filter in the yard to dry and had a soccer ball in the yard. When I went to play with JW, the mentally challenged boy next door, the ball was gone! He had put it in his shed so we couldn't play. Later that night I couldn't find the filter, so I asked him if he has seen it. He said no, he didn't know what I was talking about, and then I accused him of taking it.

He started yelling at me, saying, "Why would I take your thing, Landon? I don't even know what you're talking about! Leave my room!"

I did and went and grabbed the keys and flashlight and was determined to find it in the trash barrel or his shed. It was in his shed, the first place I looked. I came back in and said, "No worries, Granddad, I found it! It was in the yard. It must have blown down!" I did not want him to say I intruded on his territory to defend the fact he lied!

I said, "I'm sorry, Granddad, I should have known you are not that mean and that you would not have lied to me." I don't know why I played a guilt trip, as I know it has no effect on him! He truly is a miserable and mean-spirited soul.☹

Today was a bad day. I woke up to Mother and Grandfather arguing again, nothing out of the usual, as he usually starts something in the morning and at night. The thing that is different today is that he could not argue back too well. He started an argument and went into "Mad Buddy" mode, where he couldn't logically argue well.

I said, "Why do you hate me so much? Is it because you're scared?"

He yelled back and said, "I don't want you eating my food, and I don't want yours. Keep it separate! I said, yes sir. He then said, "You're not touching my car, and I'm not touching my car!"

I said, "You mean my car?"

He said, "I mean my car, damnit!"

I chewed into him slightly about how he could not be positive, how he was controlling, and how he had no friends or family because of these attributes. I said we love him and that he shouldn't be so mean to the only people he has in this world. The really strange thing is he didn't argue back much like he always does. He actually looked and acted mentally handicapped for the first time since I noticed symptoms a few months ago. It makes me wonder if the disease is progressing at a faster rate.

He told me he didn't want me in his house, and I said I would not abandon my mother and that I was the only reason she was getting better, but that I would confine myself to my room, as he requested. I spent the morning in my room and my mother hers.

He watched daytime soap operas and just stared at the screen (he doesn't watch soaps).

About 2 p.m. I asked my mother to warn him that we were going to do her physical therapy. We worked out until three thirty and he went outside. After we did her therapy, we stayed in the living room, determined to be a family. He picked flowers from the yard (the first nice gesture in a super long time) and put them in a vase and gave them to Mother. He then watched television with us, and it was a nice, peaceful and silent family night. He cooked himself a pizza and went to watch the race in his room. Later that night, Mother went to tell him she loved him and talk like she does every night, and after she said, "I love you, Daddy."

He replied, "Did you come to apologize?"

She said, "No, for what?"

He said for hiding the bread and bananas, and she replied that he told me to keep our food separate this morning and I did. He replied I did not say any such thing! He's always right and I'm always wrong! They started arguing, and I went down to tell her to go to her room and not argue. I went in and asked him if he wanted me to shut his door as I had put the oven on self-clean and it was smoky in the house.

He did not reply, and I said, "You still not talking to me, buddy?"

He said, "I got nothing to say you, Landon!"

I said, "Granddad, do you not remember the conversation this morning, or are you just lying because you want to be right and eat bread?"

He said, "I never said that, damnit." And then he talked about how my mother doesn't love him and that she had showed it tonight!

I said, "She loves you with all of her heart, as do I!"

He said, "She clings to you like you are always right!"

I said, "She clings to me because I am a positive force in her life and I bring her happiness, like you did when you bought her flowers today! You should do more nice things, and she would cling to you more! All you seem to do is dwell on negative things and argue. It is killing her, and that's why she clings to me! Try being a positive person, and she will cling to you again, but why would she cling to someone that always brings her down?"

He got up and shut the door in my face! Five minutes later he came down to the living room and yelled, "I got something to say to you!"

I replied, "Yes, sir, what can I do for you, buddy?"

"I know what you are trying to do! You're trying to put me in the nut house! And it's not going to happen! You can just leave!"

I said, "Granddad, I'm not trying to put you anywhere, I just—"

He interrupted me and yelled, "You tried to say I can't drive, and now you're trying to make me sound crazy!"

I said, "No sir, I voiced an opinion for my mother's safety, and you have hated me ever since! No one is trying to put you anywhere! You belong with us and we love you."

"You're trying to make me out to be crazy, and it's not going to happen! I don't want your damn bread. I wouldn't eat it in a hundred years! And don't think you are going to use MY kindling to build a fire tonight like you did last night! (I built a fire last night so my mother could watch the Oscars for the first time in eighteen years! She really enjoyed it ☺.)

I said, "Yes, sir," and he stormed back to his room! I'm really scared as I think this disease is advancing at an alarming rate and he is getting really angry! My sister and James, our neighbor, didn't see it and think we are overreacting. My mother says it has been this way for two years now, and I must say I never saw it until I moved in! It was maybe 10 to 20 percent of the time in December, but I see it about 20 to 35 percent of the time now—an alarming rate of increase. If this started two years ago, it was rising at about 5 to 10 percent a year, and we have had an approximate 10 to 25 percent jump in a few months! I don't know what we are going to do. Mother would never stand up to him, and I never stood up to him and still don't except when it comes to the car and my mother's safety. I never told him he couldn't do something or couldn't drive, which was probably a mistake, as he could hurt someone, and then we could get sued for everything we have! But I do not want to anger him, and I'm not a doctor, so who am I to take his keys away or tell him what to do?

He brought up a good point when he said he never had a wreck with my mother in the car.

I countered with, "Well she never got cancer from smoking, but does that mean she should start back?"

He has not driven the car since I said that, so I don't know why he hates me so much. I do see that everything is a competition to him. He will come in and ask my mother who she is going to ride with, me or him? Then he will say you can go with Landon or stay here. He constantly points out my mistakes, as if to say, "Ha! See, he's not perfect!"

I don't let it get to me, but it worries my mother so much, and she gets so angry at him when he lies (or forgets, it's hard to differentiate). I'm afraid she will have a stroke or a heart attack. I try to get her to let it roll off, but she cannot!

The next day was the worst of them all. I would liken it to a werewolf changing into a monster when the sun goes down, slowly but surely. He spends all day outside, thinking and alone, then comes back inside to argue about something that he feels is meant to put him in the funny farm. "I know you young buck types, come in here and think you can put me in a funny farm. Think I'm crazy."

He was pissed all day long and, in my theory, thinking of ways to get rid of me (his biggest threat to independence). He came in and we let him be, then he went in my mother's room late and said something that set her off, and here we go again, only this time he pulls his only trump card, making my mother chose between him or me and kicking us both out should she pick the latter! Which she did, of course, and then I came in the room and got upset with my mother for being so angry and fired up. I calmed her down and then made a quick decision to call his bluff.

I was not going to let him control the situation, and we were not going to stay in an abusive home! I let Mother go back to bed as she had been sleeping when he woke her up in a last-ditch effort (I hope) to use the last of his ammo in this stupid power struggle. I ask myself over and over again why he can't just be happy. Relax and enjoy what little life he has left on this earth! I wish I lived in Colorado or California, just so I could get him prescribed marijuana for the three of us. I feel the tension in this one little house and have seen the dictator ruling over my mother for so long and now myself. He had taken away everything from my mother. She could not have a phone in her room, he monitored her friends, her cash, where she would go, he has targeted any threat to his dominance and control for eighteen years and counting! He even used her medicated pain pills as a punishment, taking them from her. I see it now with Lachelle, Jerimiah, the neighbors, and myself. I can't get a job as my mother does not feel safe alone for so long and wants me to be near at all times!

Back to my life sorry. I had to vent! It is now 2:30 a.m. and I am taking down all the pictures of Granddad's family and packing them up. I put them in a box in the dining room so he could see. I went in his room and asked if he really wanted to go out alone with nobody by his side. He gave me the angry look and turned over in bed. He then comes in and starts taking the frames off the pictures, saying they were his. In the speed packing a glass on the centerpiece broke and he got mad and threw it at me in anger, saying he was going to call the cops and get me arrested (all this while holding the knife in a threatening manner! I not being 100 percent sure of the law or if he could do this legally.

I took no chances and picked up the glass, cut myself, and called the police first! They arrived, and I was relieved to see a familiar face, a deputy sheriff that chased me around in my high school days. He said they had been through these situations and saw that he could not keep the story straight, changing from he threw it at me first, to saying the opposite a few minutes later. I told them that he had not been taking his memory medication, and they called his doctor at three in the morning, and he confirmed it. He had not been taking it for seven months. They asked us if we felt safe, and we said yes, of course. They told him he had to go to the doctor at 9:30 a.m., and he even yelled at me for saying "Hey" when he threw out, an obvious lie!

Officer Harper whispered for me not to drop to his level (something I had been preaching to my mother) as he was acting like a five-year-old. My mother and I tried to sleep as we wondered what the next twenty-four hours had in store for us. Would we be in another city trying to start new in poverty? Would we be proved right, or would he be okay that hour and make us look like we are crying wolf? It was a high stakes poker hand, and we were waiting for the river card!

He stayed up all night, one of the three things you should not do when suffering from Alzheimer's or dementia! We got up after maybe forty-five minutes of sleep to a blaring alarm. He was already gone. We got dressed and I pulled the car up, put my mother in the car and went to the VA hospital. He was not there. They said he got tired of waiting and said we were trying to make him seem crazy and left. My mother got emotional, and the lady offered us a guidance counselor as we could not legally see the doctor. After waiting an hour and thirty minutes, I was frustrated that we had not been called and that my sister had not called to check on us. I felt like the world was crashing down and no one cared!

He had torn up the will, and I wondered if he was at the police station (least likely), lawyers, bank (most likely), or home burning everything my mother loved. I was scared and sad and, with the exception of my mother, all alone. Then a miraculous change in events occurred as we finally got to see the counselor. We vented to him and told him everything. He then gave us the news that Grandfather had indeed been diagnosed with Alzheimer's, in February of last year! We were relieved to have our suspicions confirmed, which so many had doubted as he has played it off well in an attempt to maintain control of us and his life. The counselor was the best thing that could have happened, and he even confirmed that what I was doing was correct and my methods solid on rehabbing my mother! He saw her foot and asked her about it, confirmed poor circulation in the leg, and said we were doing the correct things to change that. He even hit on my mother twice! Once saying, "Well, you can sleep in, and I will sleep on the couch," in a joking manner, and then when they had something in common (Virginia cuisine). He asked, "Do you want to marry," again in a laughing manner.

We then raced home to see if he was there. He was sitting in his chair, and I yelled at my mother as she was talking about all the mean stuff he had done. I said, "Mother, you have to put that behind you and realize it's the disease! Something the counselor confirmed! You can't dwell, we have to be nice."

She did a good job, but still made a few sounds when he would lie about something. I recorded the conversation I had with him. About forty-five minutes of walking in the field after our discussion and truce agreement of me leaving and rehabbing my mother for two hours a day, he came in and asked for me.

He said, "I'm willing to give you a last chance, you can stay."

I said, "Thank you, Granddad, I really do care about you!"

He said we were far from okay, though.

Later that day, my best friend Ty called, saying it was an emergency. I called him back. Turns out he was worried about me and told me to get my ass up there and that he would take care of everything. I explained my situation and that I appreciated that he was worried for me and teared up as it couldn't have come at a better time! I had felt so alone. After crying for five minutes or so, I went inside and relaxed. He told me he would be down there to help me move, provide financial help, anything I needed! I declined, of course, but the call meant the world to me!

Well, it's not getting any better, and I am afraid we will have to leave, as adult protective services predicted. My nerves are rattled, so I do not recall if I wrote of their visit. They came out Saturday and had a case open on both Granddad and my mother. It had to have come from the VA counselor we spoke to. They gave my mother pamphlets on where she could go to get help, but she refused, and I felt it best not do anything as Granddad needs help the most. He left hot coals in the plastic buggy/wheelbarrow, and it burnt the whole thing up—melted right through it, and we were lucky he didn't park it on a pile of leaves or something flammable.

Sunday morning my mother woke up and went to say good morning to him, and he started yelling at her about how I hid the peanut butter from him and he wanted me gone! I woke up to the yelling for the umpteenth day in a row I went down and broke up the fight and calmed Mother down. I recorded the conversation and will plug it in later. I explained to him that he had hidden the peanut butter from us and must have forgotten where he hid it. He yelled, calling me a liar and, later in the conversation, I asked him if he had hidden the peanut butter, and he said, "Your damn right I hid it!"

I then told him that was what happened, and he yelled that I was a liar and he was going to have me out of this house one way or another! We avoided him all day, hiding in Mother's room to keep from confrontation. I even had Janey come down to Mother's room and visit with her while having James come over and visit with Granddad. After trying all day to keep from confrontation, I had to make my mother something to eat. I was cooking the cheap but delicious pasta roni so as not to eat his food. He came in and told me I couldn't use his stove! I told him I had three more minutes and that it was for Mother.

Speaking of, she heard him yelling and came roaring into the room, yelling at him and calling him evil. I tried to get her to go back to her room, in vain. He yelled that he wanted me gone and went and called 911. I told my mother to get on the phone and help explain to them. They were yelling at the same time, so I unplugged his phone so she could speak. He yelled at me and got up and ripped the phone out of her hand and hit her with it! I got her to safety, and we waited for the cops. He drove over to the neighbors and called them again, and they came shortly after.

A cop to each place, he got the neighbors to testify that they heard the screaming from half a mile away, and I'm sure they bought his story, just like they think he has hundreds of thousands of dollars. The cops came and went, and I learned that taking away a phone during a 911 call can get you arrested, but since I did it to him and he did it to Mother, it was a wash. He put the television on Home Shopping Network (they are connected, and she has to watch what he watches, another form of control), and so I took Mother's television out and put it on the hallway and put my television that actually has plugs for a DVD player in her room so she could watch the movie *Ghost*, one of her all-time favorite movies!

Halfway through the movie he banged on the door, almost knocking it down, and I told my mother to ignore it, but she made me answer it. He said he wanted the television that was in here and that I had switched his! I said, "No, sir, that is my TV, and you're actually up one, see?" (I pointed to the extra television in the hallway.) I asked him what he wanted me to do with it, and he yelled he wanted his old television back. I explained nothing was taken and that it was my TV in her room. He threatened to call the police again, and I came back in to finish this page. Tomorrow we are going to the bank to take him off of her account and to figure out where I can get my mother, and I guess myself, for safety.

Well, it has been a chaotic three days as we put our emergency plan into effect and got up early to get to the bank and secure her funds that he had been controlling. We then went on to get my car legal and spent two hours on hold with the adult protective service hotline and never had it picked up. So we went to the police station to have an escort to keep from confrontation, and they said we had to have a sheriff because it was county and not city. The sheriff was on lunch and would be back in an hour. I told my mother we would try to have a neighbor go with us, as I was not sure if they even would escort us out. We went by his neighbors' John Wayne's and Pat's houses, but neither were there, and then we called Janey, and she said the police were already there. I said great! We went home and there were no police.

We debated for a minute and decided we were just going to pack a bag and leave, maybe he won't even bother us. Sure enough, he badgered my mother as soon as she got in her room. I told him, "Granddad, we are just getting our bags and will be out shortly."

He yelled and told me he was going to have me arrested and that we have to take everything now. I told him we already checked, and the officers said he could not touch our stuff until we were legally evicted, and that was thirty days, at minimum. We were still at the point where we were just going to separate for a few days and hope he came to his senses and settled down. I separated him from the yelling match with my mother, and he went into the back, storming to throw out some of our stuff, yelling what he was going to do with it if we left. I pulled the cedar chest in front of the door, locking him in the back for about two minutes, valuable time for Mother to pack in peace. I kept telling him not to touch anything that was ours and that he would be breaking the law (as if that mattered to him at that point). He asked me if I was going to shoot him,

I said, "What? No, sir, I just have it for safety, as you told me you would shoot me for trespassing if I came back!" (I had a gun tucked in my back pants, which had come untucked when I moved the cedar chest.) I kept my cool and we were packed, and I was moving Mother from her scooter boot to the wheelchair when he came out and threw the eggs and other food, saying, "Take it all with you now!" steaming pissed.

I ignored it until he started putting my fake plants and pictures outside! For some reason I snapped (and looking back, I don't know why this was such a pivotal point for me), but I lost it and went and took his chair and tried to pull it out, saying, "We can do this all day, asshole."

He yelled at me, and I put my face right up to his, and, after threatening three times, he finally slapped me! I was waiting for the police to arrive and have him arrested and observed by the Texas Mental Health Mental Retardation program for seventy-two hours, as the counselor and police told us to do. Mother stepped in and said, "NO! Let's just go, son."

I calmed down as much as I could, and we left. Officer Harper called later when we had arrived at my sister's in Abilene and asked for my side of the story. I told him what I just wrote and said we fled to safety. I tried my best to get my mother's mind off of everything and settle her nerves. My sister, her husband, and Rachelle were awesome and supportive in welcoming my mother! I was surprised to not hear frustration in her voice but sympathy, and it was nice that my mother was comfortable, but I not so much. I knew everyone probably saw me as the black sheep that broke up a happy nonexistence for my mother. They didn't see what I saw, a dying mother who had lost the will to live as she had not said a word to the neighbors, my sister, or myself.

Grandfather threw every bit of monetary control he could at her! "You're out of the will!" "I'm not paying your supplemental insurance!" "I'll burn everything you don't take!" He never understood that my mother, like myself, will chose to be happy and poor over rich and sad any day of our life! Hell, that's why I don't have a job, because I refused to let money sway my moral integrity and refused to let having a job keep me from my obligation to take care of my mother and my grandfather! I will not be a slave to money or controlled by it! (Yes, I am aware of the fact that it is necessary this day and age, unfortunately.) Yes, it is heartbreaking to walk away from a beautiful estate in the country with everything that my ancestors had passed down through the generations because of a disease that turned my grandfather evil. But I would do it over and over again as I believe it had beaten my mother down to an inch of her life! I cannot say enough for my sister stepping up to the plate and helping us out and would like to say thank you to my friends Ty, David Young, and Petrina for offering us a safe haven and care, which were the options I would have taken if not for my mother's wishes. Mother was just starting to relax a little when our neighbor James called and told her that he had called her sister Carrie!

Carrie and her father's attitudes are what is fundamentally wrong with America as a whole—the greedy and selfish attitudes that make it hard for others to live in peace. They push otherwise good-hearted people to the edge, creating the plethora of suicides and acts of violence that plagues our once great country! She is about as controlled by money and greedy as you can get! She has been married at least six times, and we think the count is eight but are not sure as my mother had no contact with her for the last decade. If she sees an angle she will play it! She had sued my grandfather in the past for money, and he had sworn her off. She came and took as much stuff as she could when my biological grandmother died, God rest her soul, as her wishes for our family heirlooms were not carried out and now that things have gone the way they did with her husband, I fear what little that's left is now gone. This upset my mother, along with the fact that James did not call her first. I'm sure the old man told James all the lies he had told the cops, plus some, but it does not bother me like it bothers my mother. If James wants to hear my side, fine, if not, fine (hell, my grandfather needs a friend right now).

PART III

The Last Anchor

When I showed up on my sister's doorstep with my mother, I was nervous about how things would go. I knew how much of an inconvenience it would be for her and her husband, along with his sister, who also lived with them. The welcome we got was better than I could have ever imagined! She was smiling and seemed genuinely happy to see us and have us stay. She bent over backward to accommodate my mother! It was nice to see that the only family member we could turn to was welcoming.

Her husband asked how long we were planning on staying, and I could see worry in his eyes when I told him we would not be going back to Grandfather's again. They were expecting us just to be taking a break from him and not to be completely moving Mother out. When my sister asked my mother if she was planning on going back, she expressed a definite No! They were still very hospitable and warm as my sister seemed to genuinely care and want to help. We discussed it as a family and with my mother being adamant that she did not want to be put in a home, we searched for other options.

My sister seemed happy to have her family with her, and I was happy to be in a positive environment for a change. My sister was able to find an apartment complex for seniors that allowed Mother to keep her independence and not feel like she was being put in a home. She did go in and out of nursing homes for weeks at a time, just to be able to rehab daily. My sister had a neurosurgeon with a great personality move in next door to her, and as soon as she met Mother, she said it was multiple sclerosis. She was almost positive and needed to run some tests, but, sure enough, she was correct! The doctors that checked for this in the past just missed it, and the small-town doctor in Blanket did not care as the painkillers prescribed seemed to be working to make Mother not complain. I felt like Mother was finally getting taken care of!

At this point I had been out of work for a while and knew that I needed to make some money, and fast, to not only make me feel better about myself, but also so that I could help my mother and keep from being a burden on my sister. I decided that I would take my best friend's offer and join him selling recreational vehicles in Cleburne, Texas, about two hours away from Abilene. Seeing that my sister seemed so happy and willing to take Mother in and get her the care she needed, and the fact that I had shouldered the load so long by myself (back in '95, when my father abandoned us, and then again with my six months at Grandfather's), I felt no guilt leaving to get my own life back on track and maybe even find true love.

When I got to my friend's he offered his home for me to stay in, and, being away so long, I accepted, as it was a good chance to hang out and catch up on years missed. I, being stubborn, originally turned down his invitation to work with him as I felt I needed to "be a big boy" and do something for myself. I found a job with a local Servpro start-up and thought it to be a unique occupation that I could learn something new. I also saw water and fire restoration as a way I could help people. I quickly excelled and was the top of the new recruits. I got my restoration certification and went to work. I enjoyed the overtime and a decent paycheck for the first time since LHV. My excitement was lost when I realized I could not take time to drive home and see my mother and sister. I stayed on with them, as I felt bad that they had invested in me and I was thinking about quitting. The following week the owners went on vacation, and I did a $40,000 job restoring a church that had gotten flooded. When they got back, I had decided to go to a movie with a friend. Halfway through the movie I received a call and a text saying that I needed to be at the shop in twenty minutes. It was nine thirty at night, and I texted back that I could be there in an hour. When I arrived at the shop I was treated like a slave that had disobeyed. The bosses chewed into me, and when I told them I was halfway through a movie at the time, they told me, "You have to ask permission before you can do anything like that."

I said it was my day off, and they said, "It does not matter. Anytime you will be out of pocket longer than thirty minutes you need to clear it with us first! We are shorthanded and you must be available at all times."

Well, this did not sit well with me, and I could see with this rule how they could be shorthanded! I turned in my notice immediately and left the slave drivers to fend for themselves. I had allowed them a vacation, made them good money, and left when treated me like a slave. My conscience was clear! It was shortly after this that I was napping on my best friend's couch at midday when he came home early from work, in tears!

I said, "Ty! What's wrong, brother?"

He replied, "I don't know how to tell you this. Your dad passed away last night in a hotel room in Nigeria." He gave me a huge hug and comforted me as we both balled our eyes out! Now, I know you are probably wondering why I was so upset when I referred to my father as a sperm donor and have expressed my dislike with him through the whole book. I always loved my dad. I did not talk to him for many years to punish him for what he did to my mother and for how he acted sometime with me. However, there were years in there where we enjoyed each other's companionship, and I always had love for him, no matter how deep down it may have been.

I had not talked to my father in years, as I needed positive forces in my life to help with my depression. That, coupled with the thought he would live to be a hundred because of his healthy lifestyle, I thought that I would have plenty of time to reconnect. This was the toughest loss I have ever had in my life! With all my grandparents I had warning and could prepare, but this was sudden and unexpected! I was in a miserable depression, beating myself up mentally for allowing him to die while we were not on speaking terms. I was devastated, to stay the least!

Ty was amazing in dealing with my wicked and selfish stepmother, Vanessa, during the funeral arrangements. She told us that he wanted to be cremated, something I believe was made up to save on expenses. She said he had nothing and that he was close to a deal that would have set up the whole family for life before he died.

The official record is that he died of a blood clot that went from his foot to his heart because he failed to get up and walk on the plane during the long trip to Nigeria. When she said he had nothing, we asked about the assets, house, cars, guns, and came up with a big list, including his golf clubs, which I wanted to have so I could remember him, and the grandfather clock that had been in our house since I was a baby. She then told us there was a will and that she was so distraught that she had not had time to look for it. A month later she produced an obviously forged will that left her everything! Since I knew the fact that it was she and her money that kept my father from suicide and allowed him a second chance in the business world and at life, I did not challenge the will. Besides, I did not have near the amount of money to hire a lawyer anyway.

I did ask for my sister to get the clock, and for me to get the golf clubs and for part of his ashes. She agreed but fell silent after the funeral, and I never received even so much as a portion of his ashes. She was courting a new man within a few months. Did I mention she was only four years older than my sister?

After weeks of being glued to the couch, my best friend told me that I needed to pick myself up and that my actions were not healthy. I knew he was right, but I was so very lost in depression. He told me how amazing his boss was, how good the pay was, and said I would be able to go see my mother whenever I needed. Knowing he was right and that my dad looking down on me would be so disappointed in the failure I saw myself as, I accepted his offer.

Not wanting to let my friend down, I quickly excelled, and, in the short time I was there, I was salesman of the month three times, including setting the sales record for most units sold and in the shortest month, February. I was never close to the top in money grossed, as I was honest with the people when they asked for the lowest price I could offer. It got to the point that my boss, "Chief," a retired chief in the Navy and a devout Christian who had taken a liking to me, called me into his office to have the talk.

"Landon, you are great with people and move a lot of units, but you are almost last in net profits! Why is this?"

"Well, sir, I treat people how I would want to be treated, and I'm honest. So when they ask me the best price I can give them, I give them the price on the right of our sheet, as that's the lowest you said we could sell them for, correct?"

"Landon, you have to start on the left and only use the right side if the negotiation goes downhill to the point that they are going to leave!"

He then would have me show the units and proceeded to work the deals for me the next month, and my pay check tripled! Then one morning at the weekly sales meeting, he came up to me and gave me my own special price sheet that was not the same as every-one else. "Now you can be honest. When they say what's the lowest you can go, give them the price on here, okay?" After this I saw a huge jump in pay and was on track to make six figures for the first time in my life! I was also able to go to Abilene and see my mother often. It was very nice and the distraction of my best friend's family, especially Dylan, his four-year-old son, allowed me to enjoy some of my life that year. I even coached his stepdaughter's soccer team, and being around children really helped me better cope with my father's death.

I started to see a complete decline in my mother's motivation to exercise and work on regaining her strength after physical therapy. I then decided it best to quit my job and move to Abilene to help her. When I arrived in Abilene, my sister was gracious enough to allow me to stay with her for as long as I needed. However, I chose to stay on my mother's couch and would only stay with my sister when I needed a break.

Mother's multiple sclerosis had defeated her to the point that she was ready to meet her God. She would express joy in the fact that she was going to die! On the one hand, it is a beautiful thing that someone can believe so much that they are willing to greet their death with a smile! On the other hand, I was determined to push that union back as long as I could, as I was not ready to lose my mother for the rest of my life! When I was seven, I resented the way my dad would yell and argue at his father. I judged my dad and thought it was wrong of him to take away his father's cigarettes and ground him from going to the bar with his friends. I thought, *Granddad should be able to live his life the way he wants. It's not fair that Dad won't let him do what makes him happy in his last years.* My granddad had lung cancer, and after having one lung removed, he continued to go to the bar and smoke. My dad would get furious and forced him to fight cancer and not give up! My grandfather went through chemo, and, unfortunately, his last few years were spent in a hospital getting treatments and not at the bar with his friends, as he wanted. Instead of living six months happy, he lived two years sad.

Now that I am in my father's shoes, I want to kick them off! I now see things as he did, and I myself refused my mother a cigarette when she asked. I yelled and screamed at her in hopes of motivating her to keep fighting! I had turned into my father, and, realizing this, my heart broke! I try to justify my actions to myself as different. This was MS and not cancer, and I believed my mother had decades left, not years. I believed science could heal her; she believed God would. Neither of us would be correct.

It turns out that God wanted my mother with him in heaven and that there was going to be nothing I could do to prevent it! We are looking into getting my mother into an apartment for seniors where she can have a life and be social with other people her age. I will get a job close to her and hopefully have a family of my own, and, rich or poor, we will be happy ☺.

I know how I look to everyone that did not take the time to get to know me. I know I look like I broke up a happy home and I'm looking to steal my grandfather's estate. In actuality, when they dig into my life they will see: I turned my back on my money-hungry father, who could not think about anything but $$$ and who lived in a three-million-dollar house, flying all over the world like a king; I failed to lie to the people I worked for at the retirement village because it was supposed to be a nonprofit and they deserved better (not playing ball with the greedy corporate monsters got me terminated); this lost me the fast track to a great paying position I would love. I have turned my nose up when offered money to go against my principles, and I'm not ashamed to walk with my head up and thumb out!

Research my life, talk to my friends, my residents that I worked for. I know these people that judge me and look down on me won't do this, because it's too easy just to believe what they are told! Steal my grandfather's money? No, I just stole my mother's life back (one which I am sorry I let her live for that long, blinded by the greed and distractions of the big city). The most you can say I stole from my grandfather is his slave! And, to tell you the truth, I would have been his slave had his jealousy and his disease not turned him to hatred toward me!

I am appreciative to my sister, who did the right thing when the time came, and I'm not sure what my mother's decision will be. Abilene is where she seems to be leaning toward because of my sister, along with Washington State (My good friend Afif lives there and weed is legal). I am trying to get her to live near my grandfather, as I know he may need her, and I feel guilt from my family for letting her lose her inheritance. (What good is inheritance if you're dead?) I did find out that the car that my grandfather said he bought for me was actually bought with my mother's money. This allows me to feel better about leaving him, as he really has done nothing for me that did not benefit him. I am optimistic about the future, as I feel you can only bounce up when you hit the bottom, right! God will guide us in the right direction. We just have to make sure we don't get distracted enough not to see the signs ☺. The greedy bastards in this life will be judged for their actions, and I hope God has forgiveness for the thirteen years of my life that I was distracted by the sins of the world to the point that I almost let my mother give up on her life.

While traveling back and forth to Abilene, my sister and I were able to get my mother into a senior living apartment. We brought in many therapists to help my mother get better, however, with her mentality she was dead set on resisting anything she was told. She reminded me of myself as a child. Mother continued to regress and was content on staying in her urine-soaked bed, day in and day out. With her showing no improvement, funding by the state for her therapist was taken away.

I felt the need to move to Abilene and help her want to exercise and want to live. I moved into her one-bedroom apartment and tried to get her up and active every single day. I was trying desperately to pull her out of depression, but I was not strong enough and her depression brought me down. It finally got to be overbearing for me, as bathing her and changing her got to be extremely difficult. I would ball my eyes out sometimes, and others I would turn to rage, often punching objects that could not fight back. I could not control my emotions, and I knew it. My father's death depressed me, and my mother, her wanting to die now, has pushed me over the mental edge also. I know not what to do.

As time went on, Mother got worse. It got the point that she was in and out of the hospital, sometimes multiple times a month, with urinary tract infections, each one getting worse, and her hallucinations playing major tricks on her mind. One night I remember her yelling, "No, Mia!" over and over again at the top of her lungs. When she finally calmed down, she told us she had a vision of how Mia hits my sister. There was nothing my sister or myself could say or do to change her mind. My sister has never been abused, to my knowledge, and could not have picked her a better husband.

The urinary tract infections were finally diverted when we got Mother to a rehab facility that doubled as a nursing home. She finally got on a regular dosage of medication, and although I still see her pain pills occasionally doubled up on by accident, they are monitored much better. Also, the nurses available to change her now results in her actually notifying when she needs to be changed. This has led to less urinary tract infections and a better outlook on life and her wellbeing! She fought us and was determined to not go to a nursing facility, however, the facility starting off as a rehab enabled her to see the advantages of being somewhere she can be cared for, and she looks at it as a place where she can now help others.

Now that I have my mother in a better place and my grandfather out of the picture, you would think I would be able to start my life. I should be happy, as things are getting better for me, but with little funds and no place to call home it is very difficult for me to be happy. I felt guilt for my mother now being in a home and decided to get an apartment in Abilene so that I could be with her every day. I often find myself crying over the smallest things. I can't remember the last time I was actually truly happy. I want to live the American dream but find that is very hard to do so these days. I want to be a writer and have written two television series, and I am in the middle of writing an epic romance novel. I find in writing, as in dating and everything else in my life, that I am my own worst enemy. I feel that nothing I do is correct, and I critique everything I do to the point that I fear what people will say. I spend half my life stressing about things I did wrong and the other half of it stressing about my future. I must set some time aside to enjoy my life, otherwise the house wins, right? If my life ends without me contributing to society, then I will die believing I am a failure. My two books are my contribution in hopes that others will be able to see that there is good in the world and there is light at the end of the tunnel!

Knowing that my mother had been, with sufficient cause, addicted to pain killers for the last decade, I wanted to try alternate methods of pain relief. I know that oversupply of hydrocodone can lead to liver damage and elevated aggressiveness, so I wanted to give marijuana a try. To do this I needed medical marijuana of the highest grade. My friend Tiffany, who is a mother of two and in her mid-thirties, swears that it is the only thing that helps with her MS. I have an old college friend, Roberta, who lives in California, and I decided to take a road trip to pick up some medical marijuana and bring it back for my mother to try. I knew that this was risky and was careful to make sure that I did not exceed the limit that would make it a felony. I drove over 3,300 miles, round trip, and stayed for a week trying different strands, thanks to Roberta. I found the most potent and a few edibles that were recommended by my friend Tiffany.

Upon arrival back at my friend's house in Fort Worth, I felt a sigh of relief. I stopped off at my friend's and debated unloading my car and staying a night, but went to check my PO box before heading to see my mother instead. On the way to check my mail I was pulled over by the police, as my license had a warrant for my arrest! I was in disbelief as they could not tell me what my warrant was for. He then pulled me out of the car and cuffed me, saying that we would sort it out at the police station. I said, "Yes, sir." He then asked me if I had any drugs in the car and told me if I was honest it would not be a big deal. I replied yes, in the center console. My friend who worked down the road showed up and asked if he could drive my car to keep me from paying tow fees, which I also asked. They said no, and I was then taken to jail, where I was treated like a dog. I knew I was looking at a fine of up to $500, but what came next caught me completely off guard.

As they booked me, they told me the warrant was for a failure to stop for a full five seconds at a stop sign from the previous year. I told the officer that I had taken defensive driving and paid the court cost and had no idea of a warrant. In my cell I saw the arresting officers as they arrived back at the jail. They walked in with my pistol case, that had been locked and in my trunk, and my laptop. I asked why they had it, and they said it was to keep it safe. They walked into the next room, where I could hear them high-fiving and saying how it was the good stuff from California! I heard them as they weighed it and their disappointment when it did not weigh enough to be a felony. The sergeant asked them if they weighed it with the container, and they said yes, in disappointment. When I asked about what I had heard, the arresting officer said it is within the law to weigh the packaging. He also said that the gun with the drugs made it a Class A misdemeanor, which I found out later carried the same weight as a felony.

I remember being so angry at that point, thinking how I understood now why so many of the poor could have such anger for the police. In this first big run-in with the law, I saw how they treat people and how they seem to seek and destroy lives rather than to serve and protect them. I told the officer I thought the commander in chief told law enforcement to ease up on marijuana enforcement? He replied with a smile that he didn't watch the news.

When I was bailed out on my $1,500 bond the next day, I received my belongings and a ticket for criminal mischief for having diarrhea and not getting it all in the pot. I am not used to hovering, and it came out fast! They literally scared the shit out of me, and then gave me a ticket for it! You may wonder why I did not clean up the mess, and think that I deserve the $175 ticket, right? Well, when I asked for toilet paper, because there was none, I was given a few sheets to wipe with! Maybe a few feet of toilet paper, single ply. So I left it for them, knowing that they had to have more than that for themselves.

I found out another corrupt part of the system when I was released and called in to see who towed my car. Well, the police department in Keen, Texas, tows their own! This is strange, as the police officer had told me he removed my computer to keep it safe. This I can assume was just another lie from someone I thought was there to protect and serve. They got to make another $165 off of keeping my car for twenty hours. I was not fed for sixteen hours while in jail, even though I asked over and over again, and I was put in a cell with someone that had spent twelve years in prison for stabbing a police officer. A very scary and humbling experience for me all around. So to tally it all up, I drove all the way to California with my best friend's dog and a pistol for safety. I slept at roadside rest areas like truckers would to save money. I got to California and picked up an assortment pack of edible and smokable marijuana for my mother to hopefully wean her off of the prescribed painkillers she is now abusing, with the help of my grandfather, only to get all the way back to Texas and have my world torn upside down! They ended up charging me thousands in court cost and fees, told me they can't give me my gun and ammo back, made me perform one hundred hours of community service, monitored me on probation for a year, and charged me for my car being towed. After this incident I get scared when I see police near me, as I am afraid that they will harass me and that I could be breaking another law that I am unaware of. So for all you country folks out there, remember that when you drive around with your gun in the car, something as simple as a joint makes it a felony.

My friends and family often ask, "How can people do such a thing?" when they see people go crazy and riot in Missouri or shoot police in Pennsylvania. Well, not that I would ever act or condone such violence, but I can see how some people could be pushed to such acts. I felt violated and hated by the police and suffered at their amusement as they profited from the system. Yet I write out my issues as a form of release. Others fight fire with fire, as it may be the only way they believe they can fight back. I firmly believe that my life has been kept in the gutter do to the greedy and shameful acts of others. My mother taught me never to lie, and so I have tried not to lie. This one rule that I have tried to follow has lost me my dream job, all my belongings twice, and landed me in jail! All while the liars are promoted and given raises or, in the instance of the police officer, high fives by their superior!

Yeah, I can kind of understand how people refused to take things lying down. Again, I am not saying I agree, I am just saying I can empathize. I am a firm believer that if people treated each other with respect and honesty, these absurd cases of violence would drop at astronomical rates. I titled this book *Life of a Suicidal American* after my mother wanted to give up and be taken by God. However, I can draw parallels to my grandfather and myself, along with every American that has gone crazy and committed acts of violence in attempts to commit suicide by cop. As I am writing this story, I look at my phone as it flashes: BREAKING NEWS: High School murder suicide Washington State. Makes me wonder, was this kid picked on? Was he treated unfairly or inhumanely? I am a gambler with an above-average IQ, and I would bet the bank on yes as the answer. Last time I intervened when a kid was being picked on, the bully's parent said to me, "Boys will be boys, right?"

I told him yes, but they don't have to be bullies! I am a big fan of the public antibullying campaigns going on right now. My question to you is: What happens when they don't learn how to deal with bullies and get in the real world that is full of them? Will high school shootings turn into corporate shootings? I believe the answer here is yeah, yeah, they will! We can target bullying in schools, but until we stop it everywhere the resulting murders and suicides will just be delayed. This has to start at the top, with our government, and work its way down. Government and big business are the biggest bullies out there, and they wield their power without repercussion. I saw a debate on white privilege the other day on the *Daily Show*. I started thinking about Ebola. I find it awfully strange that the African death rate from the disease is above 70 percent, while everyone treated in America, except an African, was cured! We have better hospitals, I know. The ratio of infected to hospitals is dramatically different, I know! However, it did not start that way, did it?

We are privileged to live in America. I should be thankful I am not starving and living in a war-torn refugee camp, I know. However, I am not. I am just a slave or a cog in the system with a better-off master that I am no longer willing to serve. Does this mean that I am going to go on a shooting rampage? No! It means that I am going to go on a public watch rampage! This means I am going to start a Facebook page making people aware of the corruption in the system! I am going to fight back with my mind, not my brawn! Judges, DAs and public officials that are corrupt and unjust need to be voted out! Robin Williams, another famous American suicide, once said, "Politicians are like diapers and need to be changed often, and for the same reason," Why are we not changing them? Why do we let the same corrupt families rule decade after decade? Do you not think that there is bullying in Congress? Do you not think the rich and powerful can hide their corruption? We need to start over from the local level all the way up to the major political parties, America, WAKE UP! Vote for term limits and for Joe Farmer instead of a polished and privileged professional politician or rich brat.

This last incident with the law almost pushed me to giving up and running. It's the rage that is burning inside me as I read article after article about the injustices that go on in our great country that makes me want to fight! I see the Catholic Church the same way! How long are we going to allow the molestation of children to go unanswered? Why do high ranking members of organized religion get pardons from such crimes against humanity? We allow ourselves to be distracted by countless mind dumbing television shows and video games, with the mentality that if it does not directly affect me then why should I care? I am not sure because I was not there, but I believe that this is how Hitler was allowed to round up the Jews. Because nobody stood up and fought injustice in the beginning! This is my plea to Americans: Let's fight the bullies that have corrupted our once great country! Not with our firearms and pitchforks but with our words and our votes and, most importantly, our actions! Research what you are buying and who you are buying it from! What you are watching and listening to and who is broadcasting the messages? Let us try first to fight without lowering our morals and standards to their levels but by showing our numbers!

If the system stole your right to vote by forcing you into a plea of guilty to felony charges by using the threat of prison, then have your family vote. Get your story out there. Let us know!

America started out as the land of the free and the home of the brave, then we killed the Indians and made it into the land of the slaves but kept the slogan. Do you think in the nineteenth century that the immigrants would have gone west if they were told: go claim your land so we can tax you on it! Do you think lawmen pulled over a man on horseback and asked for the horse's inspection and registration? I'm pretty positive that collecting rainwater was a way of life, not a way to jail! Do you think the settlers had to pay for the right to hunt and fish?

Twenty-first century America is no longer the land of the free, it is the land of the big bankers and corporations! Think about how much you pay in taxes. Those taxes originated as a way to pay for public assistance, schools and education, police that serve and protect, roads and bridges, you know, infrastructure and things that make our life easier. Now we spend roughly 85 percent on defense, defense of a country that has two oceans protecting it and two neighbors that can barely send troops to help in their own natural disasters.

Do your own research. Google how much we spend on defense compared to the other dominant countries in the world. It truly is astonishing! Especially considering that the Pentagon can't even account for where billions of dollars went. Why am I held to account for my finances and thrown in jail if I make a mistake, yet my government is given amnesty? Why does my savings account earn only a quarter of a percent while my tax debt that I am not made aware of for three years is charged sixteen times that? The only answer I can think of is that it is a rigged system. Why do the rich who can pay get to know the loopholes and only pay 15 percent when the poor stay ignorant thanks to the lack of quality education and pay 30 percent? Why is it so expensive to have your criminal record expunged? I believe it is so the wealthy can walk free while the poor stay in chains! Chains of course being an analogy for the paper trail that allows judges and police to perceive people differently and therefor treat them differently. After all, I am a white middle-aged American with no lengthy record, and I got treated like shit. Can you imagine if I was of another color or had a lengthy rap sheet?

Ignorance equals slavery, and the saddest part is that as long as the slaves are content with the scraps then they will not rise up. Are you really okay with giving up your true freedoms and those of your children for *Honey Boo Boo*, Candy Crush, and Netflix? You're okay working yourself to death while your kids remain under-educated and polluted by corporate America? Don't get me wrong, America is a great country and there are ways to rise above poverty and many success stories, but the majority of Americans are becoming suicidal slaves with no motivation to live!

Mother was diagnosed with cancer on top of the MS. The surgeon told us the operation to remove the cancer was a success, and we just needed a few chemo treatments to get any remaining cancers cells left. My sister and I were so happy that finally something went our way! We won this round after losing so many rounds before! It was like my Miami Dolphins winning their division in 2008, one moment of brightness in a sea of pain! We celebrated and enjoyed life for a week, as a family is intended to, loved and joyful.

The following week we met as a family to discuss Mother's treatment options. This is when she informed us that she was too weak for chemo and just wanted to take her chances that the cancer was 100 percent removed. I begged her to fight just a little longer, but, remembering how I judged my own father, I was determined to allow my mother to live out her days her way. It absolutely broke my heart, but my sister and I respected her wishes and turned to less invasive, natural cures.

Running low on cash and knowing I had only years left with my mum, I picked up a job selling jewelry in the mall. It was an industry I knew nothing about and interested me enough to become a certified diamontologist. It allowed me flexible hours and an opportunity to meet people. I would see my mother every day. She never walked again and never made it out of the nursing home, but we created some memories with the little time we had left. I introduced her to virtual reality and she was able to look around Israel and see places she was unable to see physically. We had some laughs and a ton of cries. I still believed that I had a few years left with her when we went for her six-month follow-up. This is when we received the news that her cancer had spread and had reached four of her major organs. It was now terminal, and years turned into months and months into days.

She died peacefully with my sister and me both holding her hand as she took her last breath. I will never forget that moment as my mother took her last breath. She went from laying down to sitting upright, something she had been unable to do for a decade. She looked at us, and I knew her soul was departing her body. Her stepfather had just pulled into the parking lot, and she left this world as her whole family was around, but before the bitter old man could ruin the perfect harmony that was her last moment. He walked into the room seconds afterward. I had never 100 percent believed in God or an afterlife as my short stories in 2038 will show, but this was the moment that cemented my belief in an afterlife. She was forced to live a road less traveled and that was full of pain, however she left this world exactly the way she wanted and proved to me that she was right all along. I live every day analyzing my past and full of regret for the many mistakes I have made in life. Choosing to be at my mother's side for the last decade of her life will never be one of them!

When my mother's passing arrived much faster than I imagined, I along with my sister was caught off guard. Even though it was peaceful and ended her pain, and the fact that she wished to be with her God, who she had served so passionately, I was still in shock at the loss of my mother. I knew it was coming but was not ready for the loss of the only person I could truly count on. This was reinforced when my sister made all of the decisions regarding her funeral without considering my counsel. This was expected, as three years prior, when we had moved my mother into her apartment, we had agreed to let my sister make the funeral arrangements. Mother could not have anything of value on record to be able to receive the assistance we needed, so we had to empty her safety deposit box and bank account. These assets were only accessible to my mother and me. After seeing how welcoming and heartfelt my sister was, I did not even think twice when I gave my sister the jewelry and cash that were in the box and told her that since I did not have a permanent residence that she could keep it in her safe. I told her she could have it as long as she used it to take care of mother's funeral arrangements.

When she opted to refuse something to my mother a year and a half later, I asked her about the money, and she replied that she had not even touched the money! Her husband did not work for the last half decade, as he had his own business that relied on government funds that had dried up, and he was too proud to take anything less than a general manager position. Too proud to quit spending extravagantly, but not too proud to have his wife and his sister work and support him. This is just my opinion from my perception purely, and I could be completely wrong. When we went to look at caskets, he made a joke about not needing to waste money on the dead. A joke that did not sit well with me, but I shrugged it off.

I spoke up and said that Mother would like the scripture on the inside of her casket, and my sister quickly shot down my opinion with, "She was our mother, Landon! She loved us more than anything," and told the lady that we would be taking the mother quote. Frustrated but in no mood to fight, I let her have her way. Mother passed on a Thursday, the 29th of June, and I thought it was perfect as she could have her funeral on a Sunday as she would have wanted.

My sister informed me that since it was a holiday weekend her friends would not be able to make it, and she did not want to ruin anyone's holiday. So we pushed it into the middle of the next week. I was slowly starting to realize that I should not have allowed my sister full control over this process. I started to see that this was about my sister more than about my mother. I grieved in private with only a few close friends to console me. The next week I showed up to a viewing that had few flowers and many memories. I broke down and had to have the room cleared so I could see her one last time in private and allow the tears to flow as if the well could never run dry. I apologized to my mother for not being able to do more and expressed how much I truly loved her and how much she will forever be missed. I let her know that although I lacked success enough to properly take care of her that she had raised a good man in a world that makes it increasingly hard to do so. I felt heartbreak for the umpteenth time in my life, and I was broken.

The next day was the funeral, and I tried to be sociable to the people and friends that cared enough to show up for her life summary and memorial. Only twice did I smile, and both times were at the hands of innocent children. My best friend's son Dylan once again helping me out of a depressed state, and the site of my lifelong best friend Chad Locker and his son both brought a smile to my face on that saddest of days.

I was asked by the funeral director if I wanted to see the room before she allowed people to enter, and I refused, as I trusted my sister. This would be a mistake that will haunt me and have dire consequences. I entered the room and went to the front pew that was dedicated to family and looked up to see a huge family picture of my handicapped mother with her stepfather, my sister, her husband, and his sister. It took every bit of self-control I could muster to hold back my rage at that point and for the rest of the ceremony! I was furious that I had been left out, while my sister, who literally had to be brought into her life, and her stepfather, who she despised, were beside her in a picture she would have *hated* to be remembered by! Also alongside the Rubles, which she had the pleasure of knowing for the last few years of her life. I expected the modeling picture of my mother in her twenties with a yellow rose that was next to her coffin at the previous day's viewing. I could not understand how a year's salary only paid for a cheap funeral with hardly any flowers at all! It is so sad that I let my anger keep me from what should have been a loving and lasting memory.

While walking to her grave site her stepfather answers a call and starts to negotiate a price for something he is selling. I didn't think of it at the time, or I probably would have smashed his phone, but

I bet it was a family heirloom that he could now sell without my mother to object. I was angered at the disrespect he was showing and said, "It's your own daughter's funeral, have some respect! I am sure they will understand." to which my sister's husband's sister quickly shhs'd me, excusing him. This angered me even more, and I sat there, watching my mother being lowered into the ground, full of rage in my heart.

After the ceremony I went straight to my apartment to grieve and calm down privately while my sister hosted everyone at her home. I shot off some texts and emails, letting my sister know I was angry and asking where the money that she had so proudly claimed she had not touched went. I told her I expected $10,000 worth of flowers and saw $100 worth. I expressed my anger with her and let her know just how hurt I was to have everyone on the final stage with my mother except me! I went bipolar on her for about a month, much the same as I did on my high school sweetheart who cheated on me. Going back and forth between hate and love until I finally found peace in work and dropped it.

I started working in wind energy and found it peaceful being on top of a turbine, close to the heavens, all alone. I felt like I could still talk to my mother's spirit and was able to come to peace with losing her. A few months after the funeral, I was on Facebook and saw pictures of my sister having a grand time on a beach with her husband. They looked more as if they were celebrating her death than mourning it, and this enraged me again! I know your probably thinking a good person would have been thankful that his sister's grieving period was short. I was not thankful or a good person after this. I sent my sister an email telling her I now knew how Mother's funds were spent and why her funeral was so cheap and that her celebrating on Facebook was too much for me to bear, so I was deleting her on Facebook.

My sister has not spoken to me since that day. I went to visit my mother's grave at Thanksgiving. I had been traveling for work the last three months and was shocked to see a mound of dirt with a postcard on it specifying who was buried. I called my sister at work as she will not answer any other modes of conversation. She answered and when she saw my number quickly called her husband to the phone. He said hello, and I asked him about my mother's grave and why there had not been a headstone put on it. He explained that there was a mix-up on the headstone and they had to reorder it. He then said it would be there by Christmas. I was proud of myself for being calm and nice on the phone with him.

I went back on the road for a month and came back to put flowers on her grave at Christmas and was disappointed that my sister's husband had lied to me. I decided not to bother them during the holidays and give them the benefit of the doubt. New Year's, still no gravestone, the Super Bowl arrives with my mother still having no gravestone on her grave. As my patience starts to give I go and see her on Valentine's Day, which was her anniversary to my father, only to see the postcard tin marker again. I then called the funeral home to make my own arrangements and they said she already has one ordered. I think, *See, he was telling the truth. You did right giving him the benefit of the doubt.* To this day I regret asking the next question, but I asked when it was ordered.

They said January 29th, and I lost it! I sent out embarrassing emails to my sister's closest friends, letting them know that she was married to a liar and a thief! I had asked for some things that I owned and that were being stored at his house to be returned to me, and he kept them. This statement was 100 percent truth! When my mother's gravestone finally came, it was a $200 plaque instead of a granite headstone, and I could not believe it took seven months to get it right! I was furious.

It was around my mother's birthday in April, that I asked my sister for a few nonmonetary belongings that meant the world to me and very little if nothing to her. My sister, as she had done since I removed her from Facebook the previous September, ignored me.

My texts, emails to all three accounts, and phone calls, all ignored. As my rage built up I came up with many different ideas to get her attention, most of them hitting her where it hurt her most, her reputation and social standing. Something that meant nothing to me as I am perfectly okay airing our very private family business to the public. What's wrong with speaking the truth? I just wanted my mother's two main Bibles, of which she had several, and her writings from the days when she was most spiritual. My sister can keep absolutely everything of value and I will walk away. That's a fair deal for her, right? Well I thought so and started emailing her with her high society friends attached until I finally got a response from Diane, a dear mutual friend of ours. I was in Clarkston, Washington, for my job when I was told the trunk with the writings and her Bible were delivered and secured.

It was ten days before the anniversary of my mother's death, and had it passed that day, I fear I had much more dire consequences in line. I am finally able to heal and regret that I let my anger tear my family apart. My sister still has not spoken to me, despite my repeated attempts to say thank you for finally doing the right thing. I can't say I blame her for turning her back on me when I was angry. I can't blame myself for being angry at her when she was selfish and disrespectful. I will always love her dearly and will have open arms and kind words should she ever decide to come back into my life. However, I must say that not having judgment cast on me by anyone I truly care about is a sense of freedom I have never experienced. I can now publish this book without fear of what anyone else thinks of me or if I am hurting anyone else. In essence, I believe I can truly be happy now! I always saw myself as a failure through other people's eyes, but through my own eyes and mind, I am a success in this life, only lacking a child of my own to feel complete. That's something I now can work on without fear of what anyone else thinks.

I am emotionally free maybe for the first time in my life, and

I am enjoying it! The first half of my life was given to family and depression, but I made it! I made it past that hard time in my life, and I see sunshine and happiness after the storm has passed! The second half of my life will hopefully be filled with rebirth and positive energy, whereas the first half was filled with death and negative energy.

I say that loosely, as I had a wonderful childhood, minus my father's quest to raise perfection. I still work for greedy slave drivers who consistently lie to me, but I have reached an understanding with them and fought to have my slave quarters upgraded. It's amazing to me how American greed has proven more powerful than American brotherhood. Why people can't treat others as they would want to be treated or as they deserve is beyond me, and I can only pray that karma pays them a visit. I like what Sir Richard Branson said, "Clients do not come first. Employees come first. If you take care of your employees, they will take care of the clients." And, "Train people well enough so they can leave, treat them well enough so they don't want to."

If you are reading this and you are depressed with your life, try to let go of the negative influences surrounding you and know that if you do the honest and right thing eventually you will be rewarded with feelings of joy. Now take a look at how your actions influence others and try to be a positive force in the world today. Help others when you can and spread love and let go of hate. Now go out and do a random act of kindness to brighten a complete stranger's day. Try taking care of your fellow American instead of trying to take advantage of them. Try making a difference. I did, and it worked like a holistic cure ☺.

Thanks for letting me vent and for reading my story! I can honestly say that I have lived by my own rules and my own way. I have now lived half of my life, and I have seen three serious contemplated suicides, one actual suicide, and have struggled with my own demons, not to keep from suicide, as that has never been an option for me as my spiritual beliefs forbid it. But I have struggled with depression and most definitely have sped up my death with my reckless thinking of—what does it matter, life sucks anyway.

I have personally seen three families that have had a suicide, cover up that fact to protect the family member from post-death shame. This to me is the most alarming, as these statistics are now hidden from the reports that would increase an already alarming trend! When a guy takes his life with his gun, and the family reports it as an accidental discharge while cleaning his weapon, or the time that a family claimed an accidental drowning death to hide their own shame of letting it happen when they could have prevented it. The third was just like my love Rhiannon, except it was an obvious overdose suicide and was reported as a bad batch of heroin.

If we were able to shine a national spotlight on suicide and depression in the United States I think you would find that the American dream has become the American nightmare! The rich are separating themselves from the poor at an alarming rate and the middle class is dwindling. As I write this, all asset classes are, as I believe, way overvalued, and for no apparent reason other than hope. The next depression will probably be one of epic proportions, with a huge public backlash! I fear the day that our society crumbles, as all have done in the past. I believe us to be in that late Roman era where everyone is partying and ignoring the sorrows that are around the corner.

I myself am saving money and waiting to buy a house and invest until the next big downturn in the economy. I expect the last half of my life to be much better than the first half! I know I sound crazy for writing such a pessimistic view of America, and yet I am optimistic for the future. However, if history repeats itself as it has done so many times before, then we will have a huge hardship followed by many decades of gradual prosperity. I feel as if I were a caterpillar that has finally awoken from his cocoon to find that I am now a beautiful butterfly that can spread its wings and fly! Seriously observe the movements of a caterpillar and a butterfly, they almost mirror the movements of a depressed person and someone that is happy! You see, the life of a suicidal American can take many forms. It can be a bitter old man that no longer has value to anyone else. It can be a beautiful young charismatic blonde that struggles to keep up with the daily demands and judgments put forth on her. It can be the spiritual angel that ignores modern science in an effort to meet her beloved God and release herself from pain. It can be an empathetic thinker that shortens his life due to the pain he's felt from others. It could be your son, your wife, your father, your mother, or maybe a sibling or an old flame. Reach out to the ones you have loved over the years and make genuine contact. You never know, but even such a small thing as having lunch with them and actually talking face-to-face could prevent such a tragic act. Have compassion and empathy for others that cross your path and stand up to judgmental bullies in this world. Too many Americans are willing to become enslaved and then give up as the great United States of America spirals to its own death at its own hands because of its own greed. As harsh as I was on my father, sister, and America, I love them all! I know being a slave in the system here is still way better than being free on an island struggling for survival. I would be struggling for survival in either place, but on the island my mind would have at least been free. My father taught me to deal with the harsh realities of the real world, and that I can appreciate. My sister grew up in the '80s, and she is just a material girl in a material world, as Madonna would say.

I hope it was not too boring and that it may have opened your eyes to some of the reasons depression and suicide are rising epidemics in American society. Thank you for reading my story, and God bless.

Special thanks to:
Chad Locker
Petrina Kotov
Margot Rutherford Hill
David Young
Ty Trim
Anthony Rodriguez
La'La Mitchell (I love you, sis)
Brad Risinger
Cynthia Gressett Rogers (Thank You)
Michelle Bennet Doan
Deji Olaiya
Paully McCann
Kelly Angell
Rhiannon Anderson (RIP)
Samual Granato
Pseudo Nic Rodriguez
Desmi Larison
Leigh Ann Wiggins
Roberta Fox
Wendy Grandell
Norris Couch
Clayton Holderby
Samuel Tesfsye
Raymond Reedy
Gab Dela Pena
Tiffany Roa
Afif

And all the other wonderful people I have had the pleasure of walking beside in this life. A much longer list awaits in my book *2038*, which is my attempt at fiction writing. May peace be with you and God bless.

LANDON

"Speak the truth, do not yield to anger; give, if thou art asked for little; by these three steps thou wilt go near the Gods."

—Confucius

Review Requested:
If you loved this book, would you please provide a review at
Amazon.com?

9 781628 576740